THE SPIDER'S CAGE

THE SPIDER'S CAGE

JIM NISBET

THE OVERLOOK PRESS
NEW YORK, NY

This edition first published in the United States in 2012 by

The Overlook Press, Peter Mayer Publishers, Inc.
141 Wooster Street
New York, NY 10012
www.overlookpress.com
For bulk and special sales, please contact sales@overlookny.com

First published as *Le Chien d'Ulysse* by Rivages/Noir Inedit, Paris
Lyrics for C'est La Vie by Jack White and Jack Stark © Universal Music
Publishing Group, EMI Music Publishing

Typeset by Jouve
Manufactured in the United States of America
FIRST EDITION

2   4   6   8   10   9   7   5   3   1

ISBN 978-1-59020-198-5

THE SPIDER'S CAGE

Chapter One

THE INDIGO THATCH OF STARS AND SPACE CONTAINED the desert night, the desert night contained a solitary building. Night and building evolved and moved imperceptibly, one about the other, cool and smooth like a pillow over a gun.

The moonlight that filled the open door of the shack threw a bright nacre path from the threshold to the foot of a calico armchair. This pearly rectangle floated beneath an ochre gloom cast by a kerosene lantern that stood on a small table next to the chair.

A tarantula stood beneath the table.

It was a big tarantula, grey and silent, just inside the edge of the tongue of light. Its two forelegs stroked the little red flowers on the green cloth, one two, one two one. Outside in the desert night a coyote lifted its nose and howled.

In the ensuing silence, the spider began its climb. The second pair of legs followed the first, bringing after them the third pair, and the fourth, bearing between them the tripartite body, the whole mechanism contriving without apparent effort to scale the nearly vertical pleats in the calico skirt.

The kerosene lamp guttered softly. By the time the tarantula attained the underside of the swelling that defined the chair's broad arm the lantern was flickering regularly. It emitted the thick sounds of a liquid hastily poured, and its inconstant light caused shadows to jump erratically on the walls and ceiling.

These sensations did not deter the spider from its progress, no more than had the transit from light to dark at the edge of the doorway's shadow, nor the howl of the coyote; but the protruding leaves of a book, opened face down over the top of the chairarm, now occluded its ascent. The big spider paused for a moment to patiently explore above itself with the two forelegs. Their tarsal claws scratched noiselessly about the upper edge of the book's cloth cover, but could make no purchase by which to farther advance their attendant parts. Accordingly the spider surveyed beneath the overhang, first taking a step toward the back of the chair and then several toward the front, whereby this latter course at last it circumambulated the book, and came to stand on top of the scarred walnut finial that comprised the forward corner of the calico chair's right arm. Here the tarantula paused again.

High in the hills behind the cabin a coyote yipped three times into a howl that descended through a long and plaintive yodel into a modulating silence.

The spider moved. The chair arm was sufficiently wide to cause the open book to lie almost flat upon it, and the eight legs rowed easily astride the cased spine and the faded symbols embossed there, hesitating only when, halfway along the binding, they encountered the first finely boned finger.

It was the longest of four extending parallel the book's title, three on one side of the spine, one, with a thumb, on the other.

Just a slight hesitation, an adjustment to the change in the grade, preceded the starboard legs mounting the length of this finger. They passed over the arc of a gold ring, in which the lamplight gleamed like a cautionary roadsign. And soon all eight legs, rising in pairs, passed over the ridge of knuckles and into the fine white hair on the back of the hand, to the cuff of the shirt that met the hand at its wrist. Here again the spider paused over the occurrence of fabric, its two forelegs tested the cuff's surface, very like the cotton calico draping the chair. One of its curious vanguard touched the first of the three silver-encircled mother of pearl buttons set along the slit of the cuff, one two, and withdrew.

From without, a draft gently filled the room, and caused the kerosene flame to flare and deliquesce. The black cameo of an immense tarantula poised on the edge of a shapeless ridge swelled along the floor and up the bookcase against the wall beyond the side of the chair opposite the lamp, and receded. As if spurred by the temperature of this breeze drawn from the hills by the cooling valley floor, perhaps startled by it, the tarantula leapt halfway up the forearm, then scrambled past the elbow and rapidly ascended the upper arm before it paused, lifted the two forelegs, and scuttled along the shoulder to the point of the collar and the open vee of the shirt, and the throat exposed there.

The spider touched the protruding adam's apple, from which the neck curved straight up to the chin thrust toward the ceiling. It walked the throat, touching four times the jugular hollow, mounted the hinge of the stubbled jaw, and arrived at the mild swelling the cheek allows around the fissure of the mouth. Here it took a momentary interest in a fleck of spittle dried there, pivoting around it, testing it with the tips of the delicately crooked pair of legs, one two, one two one.

Its body directly over the parted lips and the teeth exposed by them, the tarantula stopped. Its girth easily straddled the entire mouth—indeed, there were legs from the thin, silver hair on the high forehead to the point of the chin, and from ear to ear. Its body hung above the two nostrils, the underside of its abdomen grazed the tip of the hooked nose. Yet, not a line of the facial musculature so much as twitched; and though directly in the paths of the three passages designed for the movement of air, not a hair on the spider so much as fluttered. Perfectly groomed, quite undisturbed, the tarantula perched over the center of the upturned face.

The coyote howled again.

A moment later, as the spider discovered that the eyes, two one two, were open, one two, the kerosene lamp exhausted its fuel. The shadow on the bookcase limned the odd silhouette of the upturned chin, nose, and brow, and along this line a forest of lines that was the tarantula suspended between its legs, staggered along the line the facial features made between darkness and a further darkness, waxed and diminished and waxed again until the wall went black as the lamp extinguished itself.

Outside the house little stirred in the moonlight. Thirty yards from the shack an oil pump, its electric motor and attendant machinery, made little noise. The bull wheel went around, the walking beam and pitman link nodded up and down in the unctuous whir of birthing lucre. When the breeze freshened, the chainlink fence surrounding the pump site soughed evocatively, much as a grove of cypress might. The pump was old, its venerable presence dated from the early thirties. The beam and wheel were of hewn douglas fir, deeply checked, the pitman of oak; only the bearings, brushes and the footvalve, once, had ever required replacement as over the years, day and night, the pump nodded crude oil up from the deep, rich well in slow, uninterrupted strokes.

The poise of the hunter and the stealth of the hunted endow the desert night with a kind of mild, impalpable suspense, belied by such a regular periodicity as a lone oil pump's monotonous cycle, and the peaceful wheel of stars above. The barn owl, for example, whose shadow flicked briefly under the roof of the short porch, between the supporting post and the front door of the shack, was a nocturnal predator. Early in the evening, perhaps shortly before dark, its talons and wings might be heard scratching at the mouth of a hole chewed through the weathered siding under the ridge of the shack, as it exited its burrow for the night. This owl could make a meal of any kangaroo rat careless enough to expose itself on the wide, unprotected ribbon of paired ruts that led away from the yard in front of the shack—a seldom traversed, gullied track that wound up and down the hillocks and across the gravelled washes, making a road that zigzagged from oil pump to oil pump, and the occasional valve or tank or power pole, to the battered highway, thirteen miles away; and making not incidentally a fine site for predation.

Tonight as yet, the barn owl remained hungry. From its customary perch atop the power pole next to the oil pump it had twice glided in absolutely silent pursuit of its supper, without success. Twice, kangaroo rats had avoided the efficient adios afforded by the beak and talons, springing like their marsupial namesake to safety with unerring agility, each forewarned by the jagged moonlit shadow preceding the owl's arrival. In the first instance the alerted prey had escaped into a hole as handily as if it had completely memorized the dense network of tunnels and entrances that perforated the crust of the desert floor. Only the half-dormant rattlesnake, not quite dozed off this time of year, or yellow-eyed den of kitfox pups—discovered by a mistaken deadly slapstick in the frenzied dive for protection—and the rat's own insatiable need to eat, spurring its forage, might induce the little creature to re-expose itself to the merciless eyes and beak set in the heart-shaped face of one of its most relentless fates.

Nor would the barn owl have missed the second time, had not the target availed itself of the free zone beneath the dusty black 1959 Cadillac parked between the oil pump and the shack. While the owl scowled fiercely under the rocker panel, unable to maneuver beyond it, the kangaroo rat covered the ten feet between the car and the house in three hops and dove into a hole at the corner of the porch. The owl flapped aloft and circled the shack, passing under the narrow porch roof just to show it could still do its stuff, then glided up to the top of the power pole and settled there, arranging its wings, to watch the hole and wait. In spite of a nagging howl from a coyote not so far away, a competing consumer of kangaroo rats, the owl looked the very model of patience.

And then a tarantula glided over the threshold of the shack's front door, and over the cupped boards of the porch to the open ground beyond. In the moonlight between the shack and the first atroplex of the encroaching desert, a matter of some forty or fifty feet, the spider appeared as an animate shadow against the blue dust. Halfway across the yard the owl hit it with a thump. The dust swirled as the wings moved down to contain their prey. But the talons, expecting the firmer resistance of meat and tiny ribs, completely crushed the minimal substance of the invertebrate. The tarantula became a shapeless pulp, with a few bent legs twisting up out of the dust, still trying to walk, the wings closing down on them.

Turning the owl's distraction to its own advantage, the true meal appeared from under the pump fence and hopped across the ten open yards between the pump and the Cadillac, stopping for an atroplex seed along the way. The kangaroo rat stood in the shadows under the Cadillac eating the seed, and watching with big eyes as the beak stripped the talons of their evaporated prey.

Chapter Two

THE HAND TOOLED, HAND STITCHED AND SOFT, RUBBED labial soft, four hundred fifty dollar, El Paso commemorative, kangaroo hide cowboy boots, with engraved silver caps protecting the not too pointed, but pointed, points, the cream yellow-white stitching on the outer flank of each ruby boot portraying a gushing oil well, stepped carefully up the worn wooden treads of the creaking staircase in the front stairwell of the Scarf Building. Each step was taken so that the 2-1/2" heel of the boot landed just in front of the nose of the stair tread but not touching it, because the sole of the boot completely used up the ten inches of tread available to the purpose, the silver tips not allowed to bruise against the next riser.

As they ascended the staircase, the boots were accompanied by a country-western melody, sung in the undertones and out of tune, *basso profundo*.

> Let's go to Luckenback, Texas
> Willie an' Waylon an' the boys...

At the second floor landing a rat, thinking that, as usual, it had the building to itself on Sunday morning, found itself cornered. It stood up on its hind legs and hissed at the intruder.

Without breaking stride, one of the silver tips caught the rat in the abdomen and kicked it into the wall at the rear of the landing, breaking its back.

> This successful life we're livin'
> Got us feudin' like the Hatfields and McCoys...

A quarter of the way down the front hall on the second floor the melody ceased to be audible, though its phrases continued fitfully under the singer's breath. Halfway down the hall, the boots paused before a peeling wooden door with a frosted glass panel in its top half, upon which a sign painter had lettered

Windrow
PRIVATE

The stranger turned the knob and pushed the door open, but did not enter.

Martin Windrow saw the dude dressed up like a dry cleaning ad for western wear immediately, because, although it was eight o'clock on a Sunday morning, he was awake and walking across his office in front of the desk toward the convertible sofa. He noticed the silver tipped boots only after he'd registered an unusually large bulge under the cowperson's jacket in the area of the left armpit, which, though the other two were more modest, gave the cowperson three bulges and made it likely that the cowperson was a cowwoman: about five foot six, one hundred seventy-five pounds, wearing an off-white western leisure suit, a red bandana knotted at the throat, a short brim stetson, red boots, and carrying a large gun in a shoulder holster.

What the cowwoman saw was a naked man with an

erection, very pale amidst brown office furniture, holding in his right hand a small jar of Vaseline. She assessed and appreciated the naked man as being fully alert to her presence, perhaps even alert to the location of her pistol. The cut of her leisure suit, the cut of her hair, her weight and the way she carried it, could fool a lot of people, she knew: but not this guy, with his careful eyes and his Vaseline.

Still, the cowperson seemed to have the advantage, and smiled accordingly, thinly. The woman on the fold out couch, however, had not had time to arrange her expression. Nude and belly down, a twisted sheet wrapped around one of her legs, her cheek resting on one arm and facing the door, her half-opened eyes and wet, slightly parted lips betrayed a lingering allegiance to a different set of circumstances. Her expression had yet to begin to slip toward confusion, recognition, and disappointment.

For a moment, the intruder said nothing. The office was silent enough to discern the hum of the refrigerator behind the door. When she stepped into the room, Windrow, expecting no trouble, nevertheless, found himself contemplating the employment of Vaseline as a weapon for self-defense.

The woman on the foldout bed turned her face to the wall, making no effort to cover herself. "Go away Sal," she said.

"Get into some clothes, honey," the cowwoman said evenly.

"I just took them off Sal."

"I said get dressed."

Windrow, following this exchange with his eyes, thought he might say something.

"Stay out of this Windrow," the cowwoman suggested, "or I'll grab you by that little pecker of yours and bat you around it like a pinwheel in March."

Windrow thought about that, and the phone rang behind

him on the desk. He looked at the cowwoman called Sal. The phone rang again. Sal shrugged. Windrow answered it.

"Help," he said into it.

"Wh—," the other voice at the other end said. "Ahem. Good morning brother Windrow, and God Bless. This is Elder Osmond speaking, and I'd like to ask what you know about the Mormon Church?"

Windrow held the phone out toward Sal. "For you," he said.

Sal didn't move, but stared coldly at Windrow. Her eyes narrowed. They were grey. Windrow recognized an undisguised hatred for himself in this woman's eyes, though he'd never seen her before.

"Nobody here knows anything about it," Windrow said into the phone, and hung it up without taking his eyes of Sal.

"How'd you find me Sal?" said the girl on the bed, still facing the wall.

"We never lost track of you honey. We just thought to leave you alone until the time came."

There was a silence. It seemed to Windrow that something was leaving. The woman on the bed waited a while longer, then spoke carefully. "Boojum..."

Sal said nothing.

Windrow blinked. *Boojum?*

The woman sat up. Facing away from Windrow and Sal she lowered her head. The blonde curls that descended to her shoulders parted evenly around the nape of her neck.

"Boojum's dead," she whispered, not quite giving her words the inflection that would distinguish them as a declaration or a question.

"Hardpan found him last night," Sal said, her voice gentler now, "just sitting in his chair." She cleared her throat. "He died about a week, maybe ten days ago."

The girl held her breath a long time, then exhaled loudly. Her head lowered further, the shoulders slumped. She began to pick fitfully at a corner of the sheet.

"He was reading that book," Sal continued softly, "the one you'd given him about the music business...?"

The girl was silent, then she gave a big sniff and looked up at the corner over her head, where the wall met the ceiling. "*Gnashmill*," she said, her voice catching in her throat. "The fucking story of the fucking country fucking music business."

After a short silence, Sal nodded. "He was about halfway through it. Readin' by lamplight, like always."

After a longer silence, the woman turned to look at Windrow. He realized that he hadn't seen her face since just after Sal had appeared. It looked different than he remembered it. She looked from him to Sal and to the floor. "I'll get into some clothes," she said, and stood up. She moved naturally, without embarrassment.

Windrow thought her most beautiful. As she poked around the guitar for her jewelry and clothes, looking under the bed, discovering a stocking under a lemon, her beauty displayed itself most advantageously, and in spite of the contraindicative circumstances, he managed to continue being aroused.

Sal apparently sensitive to these things, looked at him and snorted. "Looks like the bull got left in the chute," she observed.

"Here's that record," the girl said softly, placing a record sleeve on the desk. She kissed him on his mouth, and brushed her now clothed hips against his naked ones.

"Don't forget me. I'll come back for the six-string," she said, indicating the guitar with a sweep of her arm. She smiled sadly and kissed him again. There were tears in her eyes.

"Jodie, what's going on?" Genuinely puzzled, his eyes searched hers.

"Goodbye," she said, and hurried out the door and down the hallway. He could hear her heels on the first step of the staircase before he moved to follow her. "Hey," he said, "wait." But Sal was still there, her hand on the doorknob. Windrow was just confused enough by the way life had thought to treat him this morning that he'd not noticed Sal retrieve the wrapped roll of quarters from her jacket pocket. He walked right into it. Making a fist around them, she buried ten dollars in change in Windrow's stomach. All the air went out of him with a whoosh. The little jar of Vaseline hit the wall on the opposite side of the hall, but before it made the floor, Sal had delivered the roundhouse with the weighted fist to the side of Windrow's head. He didn't hear Jodie yell, he was unconscious at the time. But he pirouetted on tiptoe, backwards, to his desk as if to answer the phone again. Then, as if the phone had stopped ringing before he got it, he twisted around, as if the conversation with Sal might continue past the interruption. But then the detective suddenly relinquished the pantomime—or, vice versa, the pantomime flung him from its grasp and he flew incongruously backwards over the desk, sweeping it clean; and crashed into the slatted blinds covering the window behind. He pulled them down on top of himself, to the floor in a heap. Scotch bubbled out of a bottle onto the floor.

Sal opened her hand. Forty quarters cascaded out of their split wrapper onto the floor boards. Then Sal pushed an astonished Jodie back into the hall, smiled mildly, and closed the door behind them.

Several quarters twirled slowly flat, and a couple of others rolled lazily to the far corners of the room.

Chapter Three

THREE DAYS PASSED BEFORE ANY MENTION OF THE
death of Jodie Ryan's grandfather—"Boojum"—showed up
in the newspapers. Windrow read seven California newspapers a day until the item turned up in the Tuesday *L.A.
Times*, page 2.

OIL PIONEER DEAD AT 85
Vegas Cremation

The remains of Edward "Sweet Jesus" O'Ryan, rancher,
cowboy, rodeo star, philanthropist and pioneer oilman,
were discovered Saturday in his desert retreat at the
edge of the Temblor Range, west of Bakersfield, Ca.

Details of Mr. O'Ryan's death were scanty. A family
spokeswoman would say only that it was several days
before his badly decomposed remains were discovered by a family employee. The body was cremated
in a private ceremony, attended only by members of
the O'Ryan household, on Monday in Las Vegas. The
press were informed of his death Monday night.

O'Ryan began his career as a cowboy in Texas, and by
the time he was 25 ran his own cattle on a 2,000 acre
ranch. He lost the ranch to the depression, declared

bankruptcy, and joined a travelling rodeo as a stock handler. At this time his first wife, Jodie Dweem of Philadelphia, "packed up and went home to Momma," according to O'Ryan in an interview granted the *Times* in 1970.

By the time the rodeo got to Bakersfield, Ca., two years later, in 1934, O'Ryan was an accomplished bronco buster and rodeo clown. When a talent scout spotted him and offered him a job doing stunt riding for Western movies, O'Ryan quit the rodeo and headed for Hollywood. But before he left Kern County, O'Ryan made a $50 down payment on a quarter-section of "godforsaken desert" just north of Taft, California. Nearly forty years later, asked about the purchase, O'Ryan said, "Sweet Jesus, I thought it was the prettiest land I'd ever seen. It reminded me of Texas, but you just can't find any place in Texas with that much creosote bush on it. It was downright green. I thought that little piece of real estate was just about the most *lush* country I'd ever laid eyes on. Figured if Hollywood didn't work out, I could always herd tarantulas."

O'Ryan went on to spend twelve years in Hollywood, working in over 25 western and adventure films. "The only lines I ever got paid to speak was *Eeyah* and *Argh*," he told the *Times* in 1970.

By 1947, O'Ryan had remarried, his Hollywood career had stagnated, and he felt he was "too old to be falling off horses for a living." He and his wife packed up and headed for the desert. Driving through Taft, they noticed a new structure on a hillside just east of town, and stopped to inquire about it. "Was a wood oil derrick," he recalled for the *Times*. "Greasy feller called Hardpan was standing next to it. We got to talkin'."

According to Hughes Tool Co. records, in 1960 O'Ryan Petroleum had 29 wells producing on the original quarter section, and owned or operated 75 wells under a variety of other arrangements, including leases in Texas, Oklahoma, the Gulf of Mexico, and California coastal sites.

In 1970, O'Ryan established Petrofoundlings, a philanthropic organization widely known for its Old Welldriller's Home "for fellers too pooped to poke" and the Old Stuntmen's Home "for fellers too brittle to fall," both located in the Los Angeles area, as well as worldwide charitable endeavors.

To the end of his life, O'Ryan preferred the simple existence afforded by his two-room shack located in the foothills on his original oil property. Though electricity runs to every pump and well in the valley, he never had electricity installed in his home there. He preferred to read Greek philosophers and Latin poets by lamplight, and to live without "godforsaken modern gadgetry," except for his Cadillac. "You ever see a cowboy didn't want a Cadillac? Any butt ever sat a mean horse don't want to do without one, or maybe two of 'em, one for each bun."

Why was O'Ryan known as Sweet Jesus? Long time friend and employee Hardpan, who would not give his last name ("I got one, but I can't pronounce it."), told the *Times*, "Ever time a well'd come in, whether he was standin' on top of it, like the early days, gettin covered with s——, or in the penthouse office, in downtown

L.A., knee deep in likewise, I reckon, he'd throw his hat or a monkey wrench or a secretary just as far as he could, and holler, 'Sweet Jesus.' No, I never knowed him to go to church, 'less he was gettin' married."

Edward O'Ryan is survived by a daughter by his second marriage, Mrs. Kitty Larkin, of Malibu, Ca., and his granddaughter, country-western singer Jodie Ryan, of San Francisco. His third wife, Pamela Neil, divorced from Mr. O'Ryan in 1975, also lives in the Bay Area.

Windrow spun his desk chair around to face the window, put his feet up on the sill. The venetian blind lay in a heap in the corner, against the lower drawer of the file cabinet. He crossed his ankles one way, then another. He readjusted his sunglasses. He sighed. He let his feet down with a bang, stood, and paced to the office door, where he paused. Her guitar and case were on top of the refrigerator. He hadn't heard from her. No doubt that, now, she could afford a spare. He would have time to teach himself how to play a mazurka in E flat before she called for this instrument. He kicked the bottom of the refrigerator. Desultory? Not at all. The thin protective grill clattered off the bottom of the refrigerator and lay at his feet. He stood with his hands in his pockets, staring at it. Nondesultory. Oh for a desultory mind randomly flipping from thought to thought, like a severed lizard's tail in a box of matches. Leaps. Hmph. Squat frogmind emits the lovemad croak and uncoils its rear legs, airborn, plop, into the same ontological topography as before: mud. Emotional mud.

Must be my diet, Windrow thought: short on protein and ruffage. He opened the refrigerator and inspected its contents. These amounted, in short, to a serious indictment of his personal nutrition. From the corroded and empty shelves of the old Kelvinator he extracted the ingredients of his breakfast. He poured a dark Mexican beer into a glass and broke a brown egg into it. He garnished the sepia barm with a dilapidated sprig of flaccid parsley, and drank. Ahh. He smacked his lips, chewed the parsley, and Pow, his mind made the leap. He paced back to the window.

He'd first met Jodie Ryan on a television shoot on the Embarcadero. He'd been hired to find one of the gypsy crewmen working the production. Seeing Windrow, the startled subject fell off a pier into the bay and nearly drowned. Seeing Windrow and the shivering subject gave Jodie Ryan a distinctly bad taste for Windrow's person, and they'd had a swell time ever since. This is to say, she'd call whenever she was in town and had nothing else to do, which occurred about every three months. Every three months was just often enough to keep Windrow interested, but not often enough for the affair to get respectable. However, he'd howled at the moon from beneath Coit Tower one night, and she'd sat up in the covers of the convertible sofa early one morning and composed a song for him.

The song was titled: "Stealin' Eyes."

So it must be love.

Right?

Windrow stared out his window, his head to one side, and blew air past his lips, making them flap. He could see a woman in the door of the grocery across Folsom Street. She was black, wore stacked heels, black mesh stockings, a bright scarlet blouse, a white skirt slit way up the front. She got a light for a long, brown cigarette from another woman, one of two who exited the grocery and joined her. Of these two, one was white, the other black, both dressed more or less similarly to the first. The second black woman held a large package in her arms. She took leave of the other two and crossed the street. Windrow heard and felt the street door of the Scarf Building open and crash shut, two stories below.

He sipped his breakfast. The obituary yellowed on the desk behind him. The room still reeked of Scotch. After a time, the office door opened.

"It's the curtain lady, sweet thang."

Windrow grunted.

"Oh, now, let momma look at it." The lady from across the street put her packages down on the desk and turned Windrow's face toward her. Her fingertips pushed his sunglasses to the top of his head and probed the yellowing black and blue bruise on the left side of his face. Windrow narrowed his eyes.

"Do you think I'm still handsome, baby?" he said.

Sister Opium Jade leveled her brown almond eyes with his. In her stacked heels, she stood as tall as Windrow. She moved until no parts per million separated them.

"Honey," she said huskily, "all you got to do in the morning," her free hand dropped to his hip and fooled around expertly, "to crack eggs is look at them." She fellated the tip of his nose.

Windrow pushed her away, taking his wallet from her.

"There's no money in it," he said, "but thanks for the compliment."

Opium pouted. "Awww," she said, laying on her thickest street accent. "Y'all wanna walk aroun with your dick in your shoe for what?"

He said nothing.

"You're supposed to say *chacun son goût*," she said, suddenly articulate.

"Huh?"

"Dif'rent strokes."

Windrow growled and finished his first glass of break-fast. Opium busied herself unwrapping her packages.

"My pimp's old lady beat me up once," she said, holding a couple of yards of fabric up to the light. "Mean old thing. Tried to break my *nose* with a sock full of *sand*." Windrow paced back to the refrigerator and refilled his glass, omitting the egg and parsley. Opium put aside the fabric and extracted a hammer and a small package of hardware from another bag. She rolled Windrow's desk chair to one corner of the window, kicked off her shoes, and climbed onto the chair, showing a lot of leg in the process. "Course," she said, tacking a curtain rod hook onto one corner of the window, "all that *cocaine* I was doing had eat all the *bones* out it, so every time she'd *smash* with the sock my old nose would just flatten out then bounce *right back*." The first fixture in place, she stepped down and rolled the chair to the other side of the window. "She was so *amazed* it didn't *bust* I had time to grab her by her *esophagus*. I had it 'most *tore out* before Lenny—that's the *pimp*, that pimp—hit me with a bottle on my head..."

Windrow interrupted her. "Hey O, keep talking French to me so I can't understand you, will you?" He raised his eyebrows and narrowed his eyes, so the bruise hurt differently. He dipped a forefinger in his beer and moistened the painful crow's foot behind his left eye with it. He squinted his eyes, then bulged them. "You're putting that bracket lower than the other one." He gestured with his beerglass.

"Why honey," said Opium. "That's because this here *Scarf* Building runs *uphill* to the *left*. Besides," she turned and glowered at him, "if I didn't put these curtains up, *who would*?" She stuck her tongue out at him and went back to work. The hammer defied the ensuing silence.

Windrow sat on the front edge of his desk, his back turned to the window. His stomach was sore. The bruise on his face still had his left eye swollen not quite shut. He kneaded it to make it hurt differently. Gratuitous violence.

It all seemed so unnecessary.

Why had Sal been so hyperbolic about the whole thing?

Hadn't she noticed that spiriting Jodie right out from under his nose would be depressing enough? Why beat up on such a sensitive man as himself, when a little psychosexual anguish would more than serve the purpose? A lovelorn landscape overshadowed a bulldozer job any day, didn't it? In terms of temporary discomfort, at least.

Sister Opium Jade had quietly extracted six Mexican beers and a long, telescoping curtain rod from one of her shopping bags, and was back on the chair, inserting one end of the rod into the hardware she'd hung on the wall.

"Best forget her, Mr. Windrow. Easy come, easy go. She's young, beautiful, talented, smart and white—the bitch. She's on the way up, right? What's she want with somebody who forgets to shave in the morning?"

Windrow stared at the slot under the door and slowly turned his face around the axis of his gaze.

> *Les roses étaient toutes rouges*
> *Et les lierres étaient tout noirs*

She elocuted these lines with exaggerated articulation, floating the savor of each syllable on her most whiskied voice.

> *Chère, pour peu que tu te bouges*
> *Renaissant tous mes désepoirs.*

She hit the rod fixture with the flat of her hand.

> *Le ciel était trop bleu, trop tendre,*
> *La mer trop verte et l'air trop doux.*

Her beautiful voice expertly intoned the arcane French.

Windrow had no idea what the lines meant, but their sound momentarily lulled him into distraction, a liquid jump.

"The next line's for you, blue balls," Opium said cheerily, not turning around from her work. "I translate freely: 'I'm constantly terrified you'll make some um, precipitous flight.' And then, 'so that I'm sick of everything,' there's a list of things symbolic of everything, trees and shit, 'sick of everything, alas, but you.'" She paused. "It's called 'Spleen.'"

Windrow, charmed, nodded, his back still toward the window.

"Paul Verlaine," Opium said.

Windrow opened a beer.

"Goddam faggot," she said.

Windrow suppressed a smile and rolled his eyes.

The telephone rang. "It's for you," Opium said, still on the chair. Windrow reached behind him and picked up the phone.

"Yeah," he said.

"Marty."

Windrow woke up. "Jodie."

"Marty I'm in troub—"

The connection went dead.

Chapter Four

"Who was that, bloodclot?" Opium Jade asked sweetly.

Windrow ignored her. He jammed the receiver between his ear and shoulder and thumbed through his address book. He had a seldom-used number for Jodie Ryan that rang at her stepmother's house in Sea Cliff. He found and dialed it.

"Casa Los Altos."

"Hello, Concepción," said Windrow. "Favor de hablar con la señora Neil."

"Y de quien llamar?"

"El señor Martín Windrow."

Pause. The El Salvador woman, who spoke with a Castillan accent, placed the mouthpiece of the telephone on her left breast. Windrow very distinctly heard her ask La señora in excellent English whether she were indisposed or not. He thought the muffled answer might have been delivered in a man's voice. The mouthpiece went back to the mouth.

"La señora no esta en casa. Favor de telephonar mas tarde, después de seis o siete por la tarde, mejor mañana, por la tard—"

"Escúchame Concepción chulita," Windrow interrupted. "Favor de informing the señora that I'm still a private investigator, and that I'm in possession of evidence indicating the existence of a last testament from Mr. Edward O'Ryan that postdates the one she thinks is going to make her sunset years comfortable beyond the wildest dreams of her childhood in Visalia."

Another pause, while Windrow's message was relayed back to him through the Castillana's left breast. Then she was back.

"Señor Windrow?"

"Yes?"

"La señora dice so what?"

"So I'd like to speak with her as soon as possible, to discuss the legal ramifications."

Another pause. While he waited, the light went out of the room in front of him. He turned. New curtains draped unevenly across the window. They were calico.

"Señor Windrow?"

"Yes?"

"The señora suggests that such a complicated matter is difficult to discuss over the telephone. She asks me to request your presence here this afternoon, at three o'clock. Is that convenient?"

"You know I can't speak English. Why don't you ask me these things in Spanish, la lingua d'amor?"

The maid giggled.

"Three would be fine."

"Of course."

"One more thing, Señorita. Have you seen Miss Ryan lately? This development may well affect her, too. Would it be possible for Miss Ryan to join us this afternoon?"

More pectoral translation. A long pause. The phone changed hands.

"Mr. Windrow?"

Ah ha.

"Hello, Mrs. Neil."

"How do you do, Mr. Windrow. We've not seen Jodie in several days. I was just at the point of having Concepción telephone to ask you if you'd seen her?"

"Not since Sunday, Mrs. Neil."

"Well, that's certainly since we've seen her, isn't it Concepción. I presume she was all right, Mr. Windrow?"

"Quite all right, Mrs. Neil. A little tired, maybe. Up all night, as usual."

"The poor dear drives herself absolutely beyond the limits of physical endurance. I don't know how she stays on her feet, warbling in front of all those sweating people night after night."

"She must like it."

"Yes it *is* glamorous, isn't it. Well, I really must go, Mr. Windrow. At three, then?"

"Three o'clock, Mrs. Neil."

She rang off. Windrow hung up.

"Classy dame on the phone just now. Hates my guts."

"Dial with your pinky," Sister Opium suggested helpfully.

"Good idea." Windrow dialed another of the numbers under Jodie's name with his forefinger. Opium Jade noticed.

"Tough guy," she said.

The number rang one half of a ring.

"Lobe Theatricals," growled an impatient voice. It sounded like a truck dumping gravel.

"Harry Lobe, please. Windrow calling."

"Just a minute," said the voice. After a pause, the same voice said, "Lobe here."

"You should at least put it on hold," Windrow said.

"You mean like this?" Lobe said. Windrow heard a click and found his ear in the middle of an orchestral arrangement of Old Man River. He waited a minute. Abruptly, the tune ended and the tape began to hiss a brassy rendition of

There's No Business (Like Show Business). He severed the connection and dialed again.

"Lobe Theatricals."

"Mr. Lobe, please."

"Who's calling, please?"

"Ronald Reagan."

"Just a moment, please." There followed a click, three seconds of Muzak, same tune, and another click.

"Ronnie! Baby! You got the part!"

Windrow sighed. "Look, Lobe. I'm a busy man. You seen Jodie Ryan lately?"

"Try the chitterling circuit, Windrow. Third dive after the national forest."

"Got a name?

"Don't know. Could be the Dew Drop Inn; or maybe Fly Inn, the Drive Inn, the Steppe Inn, the Lumber On Inn, the Be Inn, the Put It Inn, the Is It Inn? or the just plain It's Inn. Forty bucks a night, her and the guitar. Acoustic, electric or both. All standard tunes with a few originals mixed in for the over-twelve drinkers. And confidentially," Lobe lowered his voice, "spring for nice accommodations and a good tip and you get the *whole act*. Get me? Har har." Through the telephone wire Windrow could hear the lascivious wink and feel the sharkskin elbow digging for his ribs.

"What's her schedule, Lobe?"

"Hey, you wanna hear a good cop joke? *Martin Windrow*. Har har har."

Windrow said nothing. Lobe spent most of his time exhibiting his calloused brand of affection to the female talent who tried to work for him. Lobe was in fact a legitimate booking agent, but the other telephone in his office rang to a number listed in the yellow pages as an escort service.

Pimping had gotten Lobe started in the modeling and finally the booking business, and in these he had marginally succeeded. But he'd never shaken the habit of ordering women around at one hundred dollars an hour minus his percentage and he'd never arrived at being financially independent of others doing it with his women. So he was still a pimp. That was okay. But when the talent from his booking operations refused to act like the talent from the escort service, he became acrimonious. Frequently, it was a long time before the legitimate actress or singer or dancer who'd said No to Lobe realized she was getting no legitimate work because her own agent was turning it down in her name. Through a series of ill advised deals, Jodie Ryan had found herself in this category. Lobe liked to call his game 'hardball,' but Jodie was making it in spite of him.

Windrow glanced at the calendar on the side of the file cabinet. According to the X Jodie Ryan had put there, her contract with the Johnny Lobe Agency had almost a year to run before it expired. He shifted the phone to his left ear and tried another angle.

"Come on, Lobe, have a heart. I just want to catch her working some night."

"As they say in the movies, shamus, fuck off." The line went dead.

Windrow cradled the receiver and rubbed the injured side of his face. The harder he rubbed, the brighter the chartreuse sparks on the back of his left eyelid, and the faster they swam. With any luck and some astral projection, the sparks might turn into green insects with sticky little feet that would hound Mr. Johnny Lobe in his sticky little sleep. Save Windrow the trouble of doing it himself. A man could draw 5 to 10 for just thinking about a parasite like Lobe.

Windrow turned to look at Sister Opium Jade's curtains,

calico and hanging straight, now. She was standing on the
floor again, bent over the bottom edge of the cloth. She
looked up at Windrow, several pins sticking from between
her clenched lips.

"Hey ill heed to he hemmed," she said, and wiggled her
behind as if dancing.

Windrow noticed a strange flutter, as of the merest taste
of the beginnings of the giddy vertigo experienced at the
top of the steep steps leading down to the cellar speakeasy.
Sister Opium Jade, being not insensitive to these things,
slowed the tempo of the wiggle by half, and added a flourish
every other time.

Windrow reached under the bridge of his sunglasses
and pinched the corners of his sinuses.

A timely whisper of paper from the direction of the front
door announced that the morning's mail had been slipped
under it. Windrow backed away from Opium Jade with his
hands extended before him in mock horror until he came up
against the front door and was standing on the mail.

The mail included the late notice from the telephone
company, a client's check being returned by his bank for insuf-
ficient funds, a notice of the brief availability of spiritual advice
from Mother Lobelia Stilson, a symphony schedule, and a
Desert Sunset postcard postmarked Bakersfield, California.

> Dear Marty; Look at
> One week of chittlins and oil
> wells in Merle Haggard country.
> Apologize for Sal's behavior,
> but we're all confused. Try
> to catch you Fri. or Sat. Got
> some questions & a tumbleweed for you.
>
>   love Jodie

Windrow went to the top drawer of the file cabinet and pulled a map of California out from under his gun and holster. He laid the L.A. Times obituary column next to the map folded open to Kern County, Ca. on his desk and began to study.

Opium Jade hummed "Summertime" softly to herself. When Windrow had finished reading the article again, he put in a call to the Chron-Examiner's Obit Staff.

Chapter Five

CASA LOS ALTOS WAS THREE STORIES OF NEO-GEORGIAN stone nestled in manicured junipers and self-leveling rye grass. Every streetside window displayed the backsides of thick, tightly drawn drapes. Four two-story columns, examples of tasteful entasis, framed a wide marble staircase that led to a narrow porch and a recess that centered on a four and a half by eight foot oaken door. The bronze lion with a ring in his nose was strictly ornamental. Windrow pushed an illuminated button to the left of the door, and gave the video camera perched high over his left shoulder a fitful anterior and a profile.

The maid who opened the front door and stepped aside to let him in was short, plump and as obsequious as she had to be. She showed Windrow through a pair of French doors into a large sitting room to the left of the front hall. Here the ceiling was twelve feet high. Dark gilt-framed paintings of waist-coated and befrocked men, tightly buttoned up to their distinguished whiskers and whisky-fired cheeks and prescient eyes, alternated wallspace with giant, open canvases, more simply framed, containing wild swaths of bright primary colors that looked to have been executed on high seas in a small boat with a whitewash broom. The painting over the hearth was an exception to the others. This was a seascape, containing a sloop tacking into a sunset, as perceived perhaps from the terrace at Carmel Highlands over martinis and tooth-picked meatballs. In spite of the source of the light in the painting, the name on the stearn of the sailboat, Arcadia II, was highly visible. Below, leaning against the fireplace, a large painting stood on the hearth. This was a precise rendition of a desert scene, containing a hawk on the wing, creosote bushes, a kangaroo rat, and distant hills. The dominant feature was a wooden walking beam oil pump with its ancillary plumbing, surrounded by a chain-link fence. Several tumbleweeds were huddled against one side of the fence, and two larks perched on one corner of it.

Left to himself, Windrow paced the richly appointed room. The rugs were thick, oriental and tightly woven; their patterns seemed to actively surround his feet. One of the couches was upholstered in striped silk, another was draped in large animal pelts. Exotic, heavy knick-knacks were distributed sparsely about the room's horizontal surfaces: the top of the grand piano, whose veneer was a strange blond and brown wood with a violent grain Windrow had never seen before, contained only two examples: a yellowing ivory sculpture of an elephant, about eighteen inches high and intricately carved, complete with tusks, and a translucent red stone, set on a small square of black velvet. Windrow noticed that this velvet square seemed to be very precisely aligned with the angles made by the piano frame and the elephant's base.

Pamela Neil found Windrow next to the piano, puzzling over this relationship.

"Ah, Mr. Windrow," she said, coolly extending her hand palm down on a limp wrist, as if its ring were to be kissed. "Jodie's told me so much about you."

She wasn't thirty. Brunette, straight hair, fashionably dressed in thin trousers whose cuffs tied at the ankles, high

heels, a smartly unbuttoned white blouse, with a high ruf-
fled collar, unfettered breasts, appropriate jewelry on the
neck and fingers. She was pretty in a way that fashion mod-
els are pretty, and thin in that way, and tall. Also, she had a
runny nose.

"That's funny," Windrow said, taking her hand. "She never
mentioned you to me."

She removed her hand from his and walked to an end
table next to the silk couch. She removed a cigarette from
something designed to sit on a table and contain cigarettes,
sniffled, and lit it.

"Please sit down," she said, exhaling nervously. "What's
this about a will?"

Windrow cleared his throat, and sat on the other couch,
facing her. "There's time enough for that, Mrs. Neil. I was
expecting Jodie to be here, too, in as much as the matter con-
cerns her as well as yourself." He looked around the room.
"Is she late?"

Mrs. Neil frowned uncertainly and said nothing. Her
businesslike composure evaporated, and the big eyes had
blinked twice when two people came into the room.

The first was a dapper man in a necktie and vest with
matching pants. He had his shirt sleeves rolled just so, each
cuff turned up once, as neat as the fresh crease in his trousers. The second was a kid in overalls and a checked flannel
shirt. A hammer hung from a loop on his thigh, and his hair
was in his face.

"Why, Mr. Windrow," said the man, "Thurman Woodruff." He extended his hand. "Jodie's told us so much about
you." He pumped Windrow's arm. When his eyes caught
Windrow's, he looked away. "Pamela," he said, chiding the
woman. "Haven't you offered Mr. Windrow a drink?" He
turned back to Windrow, not releasing his hand. "What'll it

be Mr. Windrow? It is a little early...?" His voice trailed off. Before Windrow could say anything, Woodruff turned to the kid. "Jason. Take this hideous icon down to the storeroom." He pointed at the painting of the oil pump on the hearth.

The kid had been watching Woodruff. Now he snapped his head so that his hair was thrown out of his eyes onto the top of his head, and stretched his arms around the painting. As he stopped to pick it up, the hair fell back over his eyes, and a corner of the frame banged the curb in front of the fireplace. Mrs. Neil gasped and looked at Woodruff, who turned and walked away, listing boozes.

"Scotch? Bourbon? Vodka? Gin? Brandy? Pernod?"

Windrow, watching Jason, ordered scotch. As the huge painting moved past him, he caught the wording on the brass plate centered on the lower edge of the frame: JODIE I.

Woodruff, busy at a sideboard bristling with bottles, hollered over his shoulder after Jason to mind the stuff on the walls on the way down to the basement. The picture floated doubtfully through the French doors into the hall and disappeared. Pamela Neil smiled thinly at Windrow. "Thurman's very particular about the artwork in this room." She nervously indicated the painting over the mantelpiece. "It was all I could do to persuade him to hang the Arcadia at all, let alone in the living room. But we finally agreed, the mantel is my space, and—"

"And anything to get rid of that godforsaken oil well," Woodruff finished for her, giving her a look, and arrived with Windrow's drink. As he took the glass, Windrow saw that Woodruff was staring at the bruise on the side of his face. Windrow sipped his Scotch. "Thanks," he said. "Lot of stuff around here called Jodie."

Woodruff looked at Mrs. Neil. She sniffed. "Just ten oil wells and the brat," she said.

Windrow angled his eyes at her. "You're maybe..."

The maid came into the room and announced a telephone call for Mr. Woodruff. He excused himself and left, the maid following, closing the French doors after them. Mrs. Neil immediately crossed the room and sat very close to Windrow. She drew her knees up and put her arm along the sofa back behind him.

"You were saying?" she said, huskily.

Windrow raised his eyebrows and eyed her over the rims of his shades. "I was saying," he said, "that you're maybe four years older than the so-called brat?"

She leaned very close to him, and put her hand on his thigh. "But I know *much* more, Mr. Windrow," she whispered.

"About what, Mrs. Neil?"

"Call me Pamela—no wait," she held up her free hand. "Call me Pam," she said decisively.

"Sure, Mrs. Neil. About what, for instance, do you know so much?"

"Why, about almost anything do I know much," she smiled coyly. "Except two things," She made a face. "Nasty old oil wells and that country music."

"That must make you the least sensitive member of the family, Mrs. Neil."

She pretended to misunderstand. "Oh, no one's as sensitive as Thurman," she said peevishly. She gestured to indicate the departed Woodruff, then the room around them. "Why, the least little old picture in this room gets out of square, or a particle of dust gets on it, Thurman just climbs up the walls and howls like a dog." She took a sip of her drink. "After removing his jacket, of course," she added. She touched the bruise on Windrow's face. "He's a different kind of man than you are, Mr. Windrow. It's as simple as that."

Her fingertip traced the top of the puffed cheek beneath Windrow's swollen eye, the top of her nail running under the rim of the dark lens. Her touch made the bruise itch.

"Yet," Windrow said, gently taking her hand and placing it in her lap, "he's not so much older than you as Mr. O'Ryan must have been."

Before he could remove his hand from her wrist, she grasped it with both of her hands and held it. "No," she quickly said, "no, he's only about twelve years older than I am, but he's," she leaned closer and tilted her face up to his—he could see alabaster mucus in one nostril—as she whispered, "an art dealer," as if this were a significant secret. She pressed his hand deep into her lap.

Windrow wanted his hand back. She squeezed and pressed strongly, moving against it. Her nails dug into his wrist. He pulled and she closed her thighs around his fist. He pulled harder and her whole body moved with his arm. Before Windrow could convince himself of what she was doing, she shuddered, her eyes glazed, her lips parted, and a soft moan escaped her throat. Windrow looked over his shoulder toward the French doors, and Pamela Neil stifled a mild shriek. He looked back at her. The shriek had become a whimper. She caressed his wrist, sighed and relaxed. That fast. She released his hand. He stood up, drained his drink, and strolled to the sideboard. The French doors opened. Windrow had two cubes out of the ice bucket and the stopper out of the scotch before Woodruff got the doors closed.

Woodruff proceeded to the low table between the couches and retrieved his drink. "Sorry," he said to Windrow. "Damned nuisance." He sipped his drink and looked at Mrs. Neil, who reclined against the back of the couch, smiled luxuriously, her eyes half open.

"It's alright dear," she said distantly, her eyes on Windrow.

Woodruff walked over to the sideboard and stood next to Windrow, facing the wall. He sipped his drink and spoke out of the side of his mouth in a low voice. "She all right?"

Windrow looked at him and poured himself a drink. "Right where she wants to be, I guess," he said. "How should I know? Don't you two live togeth—" He stopped, suddenly realizing what Woodruff had meant, and found himself wanting to deliberately misconstrue the man's meaning, just as Mrs. Neil had done to his own remark a few minutes before. He leveled his eyes with Woodruff's. "Not my type," he said coldly.

Woodruff raised his left eyebrow and stroked his moustache with his free hand. "Quite," he said. He cleared his throat. "Well, now what's this about another will?" His tone was louder, and he turned toward the rest of the room.

"I don't really think I should discuss it out of the presence of Miss Ryan," Windrow said primly.

"Hah!" said a voice from the couch. "Silly bitch."

Woodruff ignored the remark. "That was Jodie on the telephone just now," he said matter-of-factly. "She's been unavoidably delayed. Something about a long recording session." He paused. "She was tired, but she seemed very excited. About the session, I mean." He sipped his drink. "Naturally, she sends her regrets."

"Naturally."

"Just between you and me, Mr. Windrow," Woodruff said, watching Windrow, "she doesn't give a damn about the will, one way or another."

"Not a damn?"

Windrow gestured toward Mrs. Neil on the couch. Woodruff shook his head. "Not a damn. It's her career that matters to Jodie, not her grand-dad's money." He put a kindly hand on Windrow's shoulder. "Some people," he said carefully, "find that very difficult to understand." His tone intimated that he could be a man of very deep sympathies.

"Hmph," muttered Mrs. Neil.

Woodruff glanced in her direction, then back at Windrow. "We did too, at first. But we've learned to accept Jodie Ryan for who she is, and not as what we want her to be."

"I see," said Windrow.

"She's an artist, of course."

"Of course."

"I am merely a businessman—"

"Merely," Mrs. Neil interjected.

Woodruff ignored her and made a little self-deprecating gesture with his shoulders and the free hand. "Accordingly, we look out for her interests in matters of business. Especially the family business. It works out quite nicely, really."

"You the one signed her up with Lobe?" Windrow asked pleasantly.

Woodruff raised his eyebrows and cleared his throat. "No, Mr. Windrow. Unfortunately, I was not invited to participate in that negotiation. It happened some time ago, before Jodie came to trust me completely. I've offered to have our lawyer look into the matter. But Jodie prefers to make her own bed and lie in it."

Windrow wondered if that trust had happened at all, yet. "I came here to speak with Mrs. Neil. Who are you? What stake do you have in any will old man O'Ryan may have left?"

Pamela Neil cackled. "Yeah. What are you, anyway?"

Woodruff rested his eyes on the woman on the couch. "I look after Pamela's interests for her as well as Jodie's," he said. "As you can see for yourself she's not particularly... oriented... towards business."

"Myself, I think she's all business," Windrow said. "Do you have her power of attorney?"

Woodruff smiled. "She generally takes my advice, concerning business matters."

"Does that include your taste in art?"

"Art is an investment," said Woodruff, "just like anything else."

"Is cocaine an investment?"

Woodruff looked Windrow in the eye, deadpan. "Pamela has had a mild sinus disorder since she was a little girl," he said. He turned toward Mrs. Neil. "Pamela, did you neglect to take your tablets today? Eh?" She ignored the remark. Woodruff turned back. "Really, Mr. Windrow. There is no reason, that I know of, for me to explain these things to you. On the contrary, it is you who should be explaining things to me. Where is this ephemeral will you dangle in front of us? Why should we even care about its existence?"

"I presume you and Mrs. Neil haven't married, so the two of you can continue to rely on her monthly support from Mr. O'Ryan?"

Woodruff paused. His eyes performed a loop-de-loop before they came to rest on Windrow, silently.

Windrow found himself with the familiar feeling of the fisherman who, having judged the water shoal and full of fish and cast his lure accordingly, now watches, nonplussed, as more and more of his line spills off the reel and sings through the eyes of the rod, disappearing after the unstruck lure into a fishless deep.

Woodruff smiled that smile again.

Windrow kept at it. "A will—any will—might change that."

"It might."

"Is Jodie the chief heir in the present one?"

"You should know that."

"How would I know that? I'm just a detective."

"What if I were to say Yes, she is."

"Then it would seem to me that it would have been important to her to have been present this afternoon."

"Yes, of course it was," Woodruff said patiently. "But, obviously, you don't know Jodie. She's extremely interested in her career; to the exclusion, one might say, of any other consideration. But in fact, she authorized me over the telephone to take her part with you in this matter." He spread his arms. "In any case, you don't say you have the will. You say you are aware of its existence. Obviously, you want the family to pay you to bring it to light."

Woodruff walked over to the piano on the other side of the room, where he carefully adjusted the square of black velvet. Then he adjusted the stone on top of it.

Windrow watched him for a moment. "What about Sal?" he said. "Is she part of the family?"

Woodruff smiled and continued to minutely adjust the stone. "Oh, so you know about Sal, do you?"

"I know about Sal," said Windrow. "And you know I know about Sal."

Woodruff didn't turn around. Windrow moved so he could see him. "I do?" said Woodruff to the red stone.

Pamela Neil giggled.

"It's news to me that you know Sal, or even that you know she exists," said Woodruff, touching the red stone gingerly as if he were teasing an insect. "Sal…" A silence of some seconds went by before Woodruff said, "Sal will be provided with a generous annuity by the will we're probating now. I doubt that any subsequent will would change that."

"The same for Hardpan?"

"My goodness, Mr. Windrow. You have done your homework." Woodruff turned away from the piano. "Hardpan was also well taken care of. Besides that, he owns about fifteen percent of O'Ryan Petroleum, which should cover all the dry holes he might care to sink for the rest of his life. Look, Mr. Windrow. I'll have Jodie call you when she shows up. O.K.? As for this new will, what is your evidence that it exists?"

"Let's call it a hunch."

"A hunch! You want us to spend money on a hunch?"

"If I don't find it, somebody else will."

"You're convinced it exists?"

"Yep."

Woodruff tapped his glass with a fingernail. "Alright," he said. He held up a finger. "I'll give you one week to produce hard evidence of its existence. If you come up with that, I'll keep you on until you find the actual document or someone else does. Is that a deal?"

"Deal."

"Good. Here." Woodruff extracted a thickness of crisp bills from his pocket. They were folded once and held that way by a silver clip shaped like a painter's palette, complete with thumbhole. Along the circumference of the pallette, where daubs of oil paint might have been, gleamed tiny gems, each a different color. He showed a pair of bills. "Two hundred enough?"

Windrow looked at the bills. "I'll mail you a receipt," he said.

Woodruff shot his cuff, though the sleeve was rolled up, and looked at his watch.

"If you'll excuse us..." he said, winding the stem and smiling.

Chapter Six

THE TOYOTA REFUSED TO START. HE GROUND THE starter until he knew it was useless and quit before the juice deserted the battery.

He opened the door and stood with one leg on the pavement, leaning on the roof. He felt like he hadn't changed his clothes in a long time, nor taken a bath. Or something. Around him the mansions stretched in every direction. Through the breezeway, between Pamela Neil's house and the one next door, he could see the hills of the Marin headlands, across the Golden Gate. Far below, on China Beach at the base of the cliff, children he couldn't see squealed and played. A seagull flew over his head, trailing another and a third. They glided over the Neil house chuckling, looking from side to side, then each in its turn collapsed its wings over the back of the house and dove exponential curves into the blue-green void over the entrance to the Bay.

Windrow shook his head. Hard to believe Woodruff went for that business about a second will. On the other hand, some people know next to nothing about the law. If there were another will, it would have been probated, and everyone would already know about it.

Windrow knew a thing or two about the law.

He'd just taken money on false pretenses.

The seagulls made him feel better. He released the

handbrake, turned on the switch and pushed the Toyota out
of its parking place. This was San Francisco. There was a hill
around here someplace.

As he leaned into the chore, one hand on the doorframe,
the other on the steering wheel, the thought occurred to
him, again, that he had little or no justification to be making a case out of this business. Jodie might have been trying
to tell him, not that she was in trouble, but that she was in
Reno on her honeymoon, and that she never wanted to see
him again. The phone connection went dead because she'd
decided not to waste another dime. Then again, the syllable
had sounded like 'troub' rather than Reno. Trouble, trouble.
Big money big trouble. Neil and Woodruff were the kind of
people you didn't mind knowing as long as you didn't have
to socialize, eat or do business with them. It bothered Windrow more to know he knew people like Lobe, but, of course,
he knew plenty of that type.

He had thought the street was going downhill, but the
car didn't seem to agree. It was rolling of its own accord, but
just barely. He jumped into the driver's seat, depressed the
clutch and pulled the gear lever into second. The Toyota
lurched twice and stopped dead. He returned the shift to
neutral, got out and started to push again.

It's tough, needing help, he thought to himself. It makes
you insecure, especially in these spacious, clean, rich neigh-
borhoods, where it's so quiet you can hear yourself think dirty.
There's this flood of nuance in the silence. A woman decides
to smile at you, and you're looking behind you to make sure
she's not seeing some dude back there with a tan and good
teeth and a car that starts, and she is. You hit a rich man up
for a fee for some work you're likely to perform better than
he can, and he looks at you with a gleam in his eye that's

somewhere between understanding and pity. If pity, maybe he's seen the Toyota. Understanding likewise; even though it violates his ethical code, he wants to give the detective a tip on a sleeper stock. But hell, if he's working, he can't afford it. So the moment of understanding passes, and the detective is hired to go through the trash and find a piece of paper that's going to dump another fortune into the rich man's pockets, and earn the detective two or three hundred dollars.

The Toyota was rolling again, a good thing, as Windrow was winded and in a sweat. He jumped in, threw the machine into second gear, and with a little chirp from the tires, it stopped dead.

And when the pretty girl allows her guardian angel to beat the poor guy up, what's he to think of their relationship? Of himself?

Windrow laid his head against the steering wheel, breathing hard. His breath whistled slightly through the phlegm in his throat.

He's a sap, that's what. Grade A sugar syrup in a plastic jug, and too thick to pour.

Leaving his head on the rim of the steering wheel he reached up for the radio switch. Instantly, a top 40 tune blared out of the speaker at freeway volume.

I know a heartache when I see one...

Perfect, though too loud. He was reaching to change it when a tremendous crash at the rear of the Toyota jerked the knob beyond his reach. The car leaped forward, and Windrow's neck bent around the top of the seat back. Before his head snapped forward again, he automatically depressed the clutch. In the short silence that followed he noticed that the car's motor was running. Having been left in second gear with the switch on, it had started with the impact of the collision. Windrow wagged his eyebrows and leaned out of the window to thank whoever had plowed into the back of him, only to see smoke boiling out of the rear fender wells of a black Cadillac limousine. Whoever was driving was in reverse with the accelerator stuck to the floor.

Windrow surmised that the driver had been knocked unconscious by the impact, and that the Cadillac was out of control. Putting his own car in neutral and setting the brake, he jerked his door open, thinking to make an attempt to stop the thing. But before he could put a foot on the pavement, the Cadillac suddenly leaped forward, rammed the Toyota again, and kept going.

Windrow desperately grabbed the steering wheel. The Toyota's rear wheels were screeching down the street because the brake was set. Windrow depressed the clutch, pulled the gears into second. Releasing the brake, he stepped on the accelerator as hard as he could and released the clutch. The little car leaped forward, opening a gap, but could not out-run the Cadillac, which rammed him again, over-revving the Toyota's engine. Pushed by the Caddy, the two cars only went faster. He threw the lever into third and glanced at the rear view mirror. Though the Cadillac's windshield was heavily tinted, he could make out a thick pair of sunglasses framed by long gray hair spilling down from the brim of a ten-gallon hat, these surmounting a large number of teeth exposed by a mani-acal grin beneath the rim of the Cadillac's steering wheel. The radio blared loudly.

> ...*Don't you knock at my door*
> *I won't be here no more*
> *I'm gonna find me a place in the sun* ...

Windrow pumped the brakes. The Toyota's nose dove toward the pavement, and the Cadillac almost up-ended the smaller car. With a grinding crunch of collapsing tail-light lenses and sheet metal, the Toyota's tail lodged high enough on the front end of the limousine to prevent the smaller car's rear wheels from coming into contact with the street. This left Windrow with his hands full avoiding direct collisions with the parked cars that were whizzing past on both sides, but, due to the enthusiastic maneuvers of the Caddy driver, they began to sideswipe them. Finally, Windrow realized that the driver of the Cadillac was interested in smashing him and his car between the front end of the Cadillac and any handy immovable object.

Two blocks from the Neil home, it became obvious that the driver of the Cadillac was about to learn how to control the helpless Toyota attached to its front end, and would soon succeed in his purpose. At the end of the second block, as the cross street opened up, downhill to his right, Windrow clawed the wheel in that direction, while mentally gauging what it would take to get his gun out of the glove compartment under these circumstances.

The Toyota swerved right, then sideways entirely, and tore itself loose from the Cadillac. Still accelerating, suddenly free of its extra load, the black limousine skewed through the intersection, far into the block beyond. Though he was upside down, as the Toyota pivoted axially on its left front headlight, Windrow could see the Cadillac's brake lights light up through his passenger window. After the intersection, the cross street turned sharply downhill, so that as the Toyota entered the street sideways, its nose dipped, the left front wheel collapsed, and the car rolled over onto its left fender. Windrow found himself watching the Cadillac's brake lights through his rear window, and then through the passenger window, as the car went onto its roof.

He tried to keep his eyes on the Cadillac, thinking to get its license number, but everything went green as the Toyota penetrated a tall hedge-row. Something knocked off his sunglasses. There still was, in all the noise, the radio.

> ...*Oh you hide it so well*
> *But it's easy to tell* ...

The last thing he could remember seeing out the back window was a trail of turbulent leaves and lawn furniture.

The last thing he heard was the disintegration of the window wall separating the solarium from the patio on the west side of the A.R. Maclellan home.

The Maclellans were in Carmel at the time of the intrusion, and suffered no injuries.

Chapter Seven

YOU'RE ONLY AS GOOD AS YOUR LAST PERFORMANCE, BUT you might do better—or worse—tonight.

He could hear Jodie Ryan telling it to him, he could see her saying it, so he was probably unconscious. He put his hand out to touch her.

"Now, now, Mr. Windrow. Try to save it for Saturday night."

He forced his swollen eyes to become slits and admit light. Beyond the plastic bracelet on his extended wrist, a nurse bustled about his bed, tucking in the sheets with one hand and catching his hand with her other. He could see gray hair, broad shoulders and thick arms. Jodie had gotten old.

"...just about the luckiest man in this hospital," she was saying, "don't make me break your arm. It would spoil your streak." She folded his arm across his chest, then gently took a pillow from beneath his head and removed its casing. "Of course," she mused, "there's Seamus Moriarty, in Supply..."

"Sup..." Windrow muttered. His tongue stuck to the roof of his mouth. His voice sounded like a prison dishwasher. He cleared his throat, tried again, and got no sound at all.

"Supply," the nurse confirmed, unperturbed. "Seamus won two thousand dollars last week on the goddam Pittsburgh Steelers."

"Two... sand... lars," Windrow croaked. "guess... lot of... dough... in Sup..."

"Not for the Irish it isn't."

"Cath'lic... Protes...?

"Both."

"The generalist swine."

"Junky. Cleaned out the dispensary morphine, flew to Nevada and moved into a whorehouse. Shot the wad and the bindle in three glorious days and nights." She thumped up the pillow and gently replaced it under his head.

"I thought you said he was lucky."

"He was and still is," she said, removing an empty pill cup from the table next to the bed. "He didn't die and didn't get caught." She gave him a look. "You, on the other hand, didn't die either." She sighed. "But you got caught."

A man in a white coat with the tubes of a stethoscope spilling out of a side pocket entered the room. He carried a sheath of x-rays on a metal clip, wore a tie and a worried face.

"So what makes me so lucky?" Windrow asked.

"First man to touch me in three days and get away with it," said the nurse, folding her big arms across her chest, and looking over the doctor's shoulder. He held three x-rays up to the light, one by one, and shook his head over each. He looked at the last x-ray the longest, turning it in the light until it was upside down.

"Mmmmmm," he said.

"Hmph," said the nurse.

"Am I draftable?" Windrow asked, hopefully.

"Contraindicated," muttered the doctor.

"Tsk," said the nurse. She shook her head.

"Miraculous," said the doctor, lowering the last film. He handed the x-rays to the nurse. "There's nothing wrong with you."

Windrow looked at him through his slits. Every muscle in his body was sore. He'd been run over by a Cadillac limousine and a house.

"As far as the police could tell, your car rolled over at least three times, and they're going to have to melt down a beach to replace all the windows you broke. Your car was completely destroyed, there's nothing left of it. A wrecker had to park on the sidewalk and winch it out of the dining room through the hole in the wall. Surviving the impact, you should have been incinerated, you had a full tank of gasoline. Yet, all the gasoline did was run out on the orchids and a 17th century Persian rug. When you were thrown clear of the wreckage you should have been killed outright when the marble-topped dining room table cut you in half. Yet, the table was destroyed when the banana tree fell over it, a millisecond before you got there. Nice table, too; sat twelve with elbow room. Instead you landed in the arms of six dryads on a sixteenth century tapestry that hung a foot off the wall, destroying it too. But, it saved your life. A few feet to the left, you'd have hit a suit of armor holding a broad sword and battle axe. On the other side, an eight foot glass cabinet full of Dresden China." He gestured emptily. "After you tore the tapestry off the wall, you and it fell onto a sofa that wasn't supposed to have been there. The workmen who found you had moved it there while they were sanding down the floors in the living room."

He shook his head in disbelief. "It's incredible," he said. "In all my years as a sawbones, I've never seen anyone go through so much and come out so fit. The worst injury you sustained is that bruise on the left side of your face."

Windrow raised the eyebrow over the uninjured eye. Sal would laugh to hear that. He'd have to tell her about it when he caught up with her.

The doctor nudged Windrow's shoulder with a friendly fist. "You'll be in good enough shape to start paying off the stuff you destroyed by Monday. It comes to about $775,000." He shook his head. "Incredible. Just like on TV." He looked Windrow straight in his slits with the wide eyes of the true believer. This had the effect of making the worried look a tired one. "You're a very lucky man, Mr. Windrow. Luckiest guy I heard of since Seamus Moriarty won two thousand dollars on the goddam Pittsburgh—"

"Don't count your apples, apple."

Windrow closed his slits and groaned. "Morphine," he said. "Taxi."

"You tell him, chief."

"Shut up, stupid."

Windrow didn't want to recognize the voices of Max Bdeniowitz and Petrel Gleason. He pulled the bedclothes over his head. He could hear a siren, far away.

"Good day inspector. He's awake this morning, but he should rest," the doctor suggested, helpfully.

"We all should rest," Bdeniowitz growled, "but I want to wrap this case before lunch."

"And the only way to have a tough bird like this for lunch," Gleason added, "is to grill him slow. Real slow."

Windrow moved the covers and opened one eye. Gleason, standing behind Bdeniowitz, winked at him. Bdeniowitz shot a glance at the doctor and nurse. They excused themselves. "Give us a call if you feel sick or anything," the nurse said. She glared at Bdeniowitz and followed the doctor out the door.

Bdeniowitz stood over Windrow with his hands buried in the pockets of his pants. Gleason, dressed like his own idea of a detective, buried his hands in the pockets of his belted trench coat. He also wore a slouch hat, and, as always, a cigarette dangled off his lower lip. He liked to hold his head to one side and squint the lower eye against the smoke from the cigarette. Posed thus, he could pass himself off as a thinking man, until someone asked him a question.

"Funny coincidence yesterday," Bdeniowitz said, looking down at Windrow, "out to the Sea Cliff neighborhood."

"I could use a laugh," Windrow said.

"You won't see the humor," Bdeniowitz said, scratching his chin. "First day I'm back from my vacation, I read in the Herb Caen about this 'forcible entry' out to the Sea Cliff. And who's booked on it? Our old pal, the famous Marty Windrow."

Windrow knew Bdeniowitz would never forgive him for bringing the heat of publicity down on his office, years before, but it was the first he'd heard of the forcible entry. He smiled with the corner of his mouth less sore than the other one.

"Look at it this way, Max," he said. "If you can make me laugh, it'll hurt. But as for the forcible entry, forget it. Go book a black Cadillac for voluntary attempted manslaughter."

Bdeniowitz scowled. "Don't interrupt. It's after I'm reading the front page I'm reading about you. The front page is interesting of its own accord. I'm just back from vacation, you understand." He jerked a thumb toward Gleason. "Things around the office are quiet—too quiet. So I read the papers to find out what the criminal element is up to." Bdeniowitz slid the room's single chair close to the head of Windrow's bed, straddled it and sat, folding his arms on its back. "Seems like the department is investigating a crime of passion, out to the Sea Cliff..." he paused. Windrow felt his heart sink. Had he killed someone in that house with his car? He tried his memory. He could remember holding on, and yellow and green aluminum lawn furniture, and the hedge. He couldn't remember how he came to be thrown out of the car, or what happened after.

Bdeniowitz watched him, gauging his reaction. Windrow said nothing. After a well-timed silence, Max continued. "So, according to the papers, about two blocks over and a hundred yards down from your story, there's another story, a sadder one." He shrugged. "It's a sad world. Some people count more than others, even when they're dead."

Another pause.

Bdeniowitz sighed. "So this society broad, she turns up at the bottom of the cliff, right below her own house. Suicide, looks like." Bdeniowitz spread his hands. "Name of Pamela Neil bounce with you, apple?"

Windrow blinked. When his slits reopened, they were wider than before.

Bdeniowitz was deadpan.

"What happened?"

"Why don't you tell us?"

"It's your story. Finish it."

Bdeniowitz shrugged. "Quite a bit happening, by the look of things. First, the boys from homicide," he pointed over his shoulder at Gleason, who cleared his throat, "they think it's a suicide. There's plenty of explanations for that. She had everything in the world she needed. Monthly divorce settlement, a new inheritance, big home, art, boyfriend, a yacht, and another home, maybe a little smaller, to rest from the big one in. So, it's obvious, she probably couldn't stand being alive. Like that. She even had plenty of cocaine. Now the cocaine, that's something. Killing yourself because you're rich is one thing, but getting crazy and stupid behind a lot of nose candy..." Bdenoiwitz wagged a forefinger at Windrow, as if he were lecturing a child. "A theorist down at headquarters, a specialist in reconstructing homicides," he tilted his head toward Gleason, who shifted uneasily, "came up with a really plausible explanation for this poor woman's untimely demise." Bdeniowitz sighed again, heavily.

"It seems," he began, "it seems... Oh Christ." He scrubbed his forehead, shielding his eyes from Windrow. "You tell him, Gleason."

Gleason cleared his throat again and used his hands while he talked. "Well, she's rich, sure. So she don't have to work and she's sitting around this big joint all day, snorting the blow, free-basing too. That's hard on a person. Doing nothing but dope gets your brain working on itself. You get nervous, paranoid. You think the world's out to get you. Everybody wants your ass, if it's nice, or your coke. Like that." Gleason looked from Windrow to Bdeniowitz and back again. Bdeniowitz kept his face hidden from Gleason, scratched an eyebrow. "So she's there in the house, all by herself. She's holding nearly an ounce of cocaine, and she knows that's big trouble, even in San Francisco. Maybe the ounce has just been delivered, by a certain out-of-work detective and ex-cop, a known pot offender, who came on to her, shook her up, made her more nervous than usual. There's the sex angle: she'd just had some of that..." Gleason avoided Windrow's slitted eyes. Windrow's disdain hurt his own face. "Anyhow, there's this huge commotion down the street. Sirens, firetrucks, cops; a traffic jam, ambulance, a crowd and a TV news truck. She thinks the sirens are for her, the dragnet is on and the bust is coming down. She's wrong of course; they're down there untangling a private dick and his car from all that nice furniture. But she doesn't know that. She runs around the house with the ounce of coke. What to do, what to do. It's too big to flush down the john whole, and there won't be time to empty it slowly. Increasingly hysterical, she zigzags all over the house and then: Aha! The cliff. She'll just throw it at the ocean. She runs outside, leans over the low balcony railing, heaves the bag, slips..." Gleason inverted the palms of both hands. "Good night Miss Anne." He stood, waiting for a reaction.

He got silence.

Gleason squinted. "Irene, I mean," he said, almost as if to himself. "Good night, Irene."

Bdeniowitz sighed and talked to the floor. "A kid on the beach calls it in. They get the corpse downtown and find all these wood fragments, splinters, embedded in the body, especially about the head and shoulders. The homicide theorist opines as how there are a lot of junipers and scrub cypress on the way down to the beach. The full report, with theory, is released to the newspapers, who just happened already to be right down the street photographing what's left of the Maclellan place, and insist they know what happened for the morning edition *before* the autopsy." He looked up at Windrow. Windrow returned the gaze.

"Well, we found the ounce," Gleason protested meekly. Bdeniowitz ignored him.

"The theorist—unrelenting, brilliant, self-taught—got one thing right: You." Bdeniowitz pointed at Windrow's nose, "You had something to do with it." His voice was suddenly forthright and loud. "I don't buy no funny coincidences. We got you, we got mayhem, and only a block separates the two. No coincidences, not even a little one, even if it is in the Herb Caen. As for the rest," he threw up his hands. "Shit," he said, "The boss catches a fish this big." He let about six inches separate his two index fingers. "When he gets back from his vacation and his taxidermist, the boss is in shock to discover the city is still where he'd left it, with people walking around in it. In spite of his condition he goes to work. Upon reading the papers concerning the preceding events, and after auditioning theories, the boss fires everybody and orders a routine analysis of the cause of death." Bdeniowitz read the palm of one hand with the forefinger of the other, squinting as if farsighted. "Hmm. Multiple contusions and abrasions about the head and shoulders of the deceased, many of them thought to have been caused by a blunt instrument. The wood splinters embedded in the deceased turn out to be spruce and mahogany. Well, well!" Bdeniowitz shot Gleason a look of contempt. His voice transuded sarcasm. "Further investigation, conducted both in our modern forensic laboratories and at the scene of the crime by our highly trained and skilled personnel, revealed some interesting *facts*. No investigation is complete without a couple of *facts*." He enumerated his fingers. "The smashed remains of a stringed instrument, possibly a guitar, strewn on the rocks below the house, and its neck—with the strings still on it, not far away, trapped in the junipers about halfway down the cliff. There's blood on both. Analysis revealed the blood was of exactly the same type as the victim's. Well, well, whaddya know. Now it's a homicide, with dope, sex, and music thrown in."

Windrow started to speak. Bdeniowitz held up a hand and shook his head.

"Then what do we find? Various drink glasses around the house, each containing residues of various expensive boozes. All of the beautifully defined fingerprints on these glasses can be accounted for by comparing them with those of the residents or servants pertaining to the premises. All, that is, except for one lovely thumbprint, which, lo and behold, turns out to belong to an ex-cop, one Martin Windrow, last seen, more dead than alive, on page twenty-one, next to the Macy's ad, left hand gossip column, 'breaking and entering'." Bdeniowitz paused.

"But not as dead as the deceased," he added quietly.

Another silence.

"You had scotch, Marty," Gleason said.

Chapter Eight

WINDROW LOOKED AT THE SUNLIGHT STREAMING through the hospital window and wished he were part of it. If so, he would swim upstream a few miles. High above the city he could bounce a sunbeam off a cup of coffee into a sad man's face, sure, and he could follow black limousines through the streets, watch a body plunge down a cliff, follow an elusive singer to her telephone, spot the red roll of quarters through that tiny window in that huge array of windows, there, the two cops badgering the sick man in his bed, and warm their backs for them, make them less assiduous. Of course, light changes everything; light is information. And information is light; but whereas the sun provides warmth, the fact of the death of Pamela Neil chilled decidedly the atmosphere in the room.

The siren got real loud as it approached the base of the hospital building, and stopped.

Bdeniowitz was oddly patient. Windrow looked at him. "Did you check her for residual cocaine?"

Bdeniowitz made a wagging motion with the fingers of his upturned palm. "The story the story," he said. "Let's have it."

"I was there. I was just leaving her house when this Cadillac limousine..."

"Wait a minute, wait a minute. What were you doing at this dame's house? Delivering laundry?"

"I was looking for her step-daughter."

Bdeniowitz looked at Gleason and whistled. "Her step-daughter. this Neil was maybe thirty. She..."

"Twenty-nine," Windrow said.

Bdeniowitz looked back at him. "Gleason," he said. Petrel Gleason thumbed through a pocket-sized spiral notebook. Bdeniowitz didn't wait. "Twenty-nine, thirty. So how old's the daughter, Windrow? Fourteen? Twelve?"

"The Mann Act," Gleason chuckled, still thumbing through the narrow pages. "Breaking and entering, willful destruction of private property, *the Mann Act*..."

"About the same," Windrow sighed.

The two cops looked at him.

"She's twenty-seven, for chrissake."

"Old enough to bite," Gleason observed.

"She's a friend of mine," said Windrow. "She travels when she works, which is all the time, so she doesn't maintain an apartment anywhere. When she's in town, she stays with her stepmother."

"So you went over there to see her."

"Yeah. Only there was some kind of foul up. She wasn't home. She got hung up working. So I sat down and had a drink with Mrs. Neil and the aesthete she lives with."

"Twenty-nine," Gleason announced, reading from his notebook.

"Ass-theet?" said Bdeniowitz.

"Right," said Windrow. "Name of Woodruff. Collects art." Gleason raised an eyebrow and begun thumbing through his notebook again. "I had a scotch," Windrow recalled. Gleason paused, then reversed his way through the pages and stopped. "Scotch," he said. "Woodruff," Windrow said. Gleason began to go the other way through his notebook. "Talked about the weather for a while. Mrs. Neil's nose was running, seems she's had sinus since they left Palm Springs. It's the fog. Like that. While we were talking Jodie called and said she'd be delayed. You might check on that call, as a matter of fact, if you can. I'd be interested in that."

"Oh, we might check on that call for you, eh?" snarled Bdeniowitz. "What else happened?"

"What else? Nothing else. I finished my drink and left."

"What did you talk about? The maid said you stayed for the better part of an hour."

"Well, that's her story. They kept me waiting fifteen minutes after I got there. Then there was some business about a painting they were hanging. You probably saw a sailboat over the mantlepiece when you got there? That—"

"Wait a minute," Bdeniowitz frowned. "Hold it. Gleason."

"Woodruff," Gleason said, holding a finger in the air and looking at his notebook.

Bdeniowitz shook his head.

"Goddam it Gleason," he said quietly. "Go call O'Shaunessy at the Neil house. Get him to describe the painting that's hanging over the fireplace in the living room."

"Right back, chief," Gleason said. He waved the notebook. "I got the number right here." He left the room.

Bdeniowitz turned back to Windrow. A puzzled frown lingered on his face. "Sailboat," he muttered. "So what else?"

Windrow shrugged and partially closed up his left eye, screwing up the outside corner of it, so that the bruise stung around it. But the competition for his nervous system's attention was fierce. "Let's see. There was a kid there, helping to move the painting. Name of Jason. Young guy, wore coveralls and carried a hammer. His hair was in his face all the time."

"We talked to him. Dumb as a post."

"Dumb as a—"

"Can't talk and, he's deaf, too. Reads lips and speaks in sign language. Claims he didn't notice anything unusual yesterday, outside the ordinary squabbling."

Windrow remembered how the kid had watched Woodruff. It annoyed him that he hadn't noticed why.

"They scrapped a lot?"

"All the time, according to the kid. The maid confirmed it. He didn't mention anything about a painting, though. What else?"

"Well, about the time we're through with the pleasantries the maid comes in and says there's a phone call. Woodruff goes out and takes it."

"Wait. Don't tell me. While he's out of the room the missus jumps you. She says she and the old man aren't making it anymore, and it's been a long time since there's been a real man around the house..."

"That was the last case," Windrow said, grinding his teeth.

"Oh." Bdeniowitz lapsed back into his slightly puzzled state. "So did she say anything?"

Windrow shook his head. "Not much," he said. "She was pretty stoned. Stared a lot, made a couple of obtuse remarks and sniffled once in a while. I finished my drink and she told me to help myself to another. I was doing that when Woodruff came back and told me Jodie had called."

"Driving drunk, eh? So who's this Jodie?"

"That's the stepdaughter."

"Oh, yeah, I forgot."

Bdeniowitz paused for a moment before his next question.

"When did you realize she was Sweet Jesus O'Ryan's granddaughter?"

Windrow almost permitted himself a smile. Max was never as ignorant as he pretended to be.

"When I read about it in the papers, same as you."

"She never mentioned him?"

"Never."

"So what happened to her?"

"Woodruff told me she's in a recording session, and running late. He said she's real excited about the session, apologetic about our date, and that she'll be in touch."

"So how come she didn't ask the maid for you?"

"That's a good question." Windrow didn't mention that he hadn't believed for one minute that the Ryan girl had been on the telephone at all. He said, "I'll have to ask her that when I see her," and Bdeniowitz nodded.

Gleason came back in the room. "I got a hold of O'Shaunessey," he said. "Says there's a painting of an oil pump over the fireplace. An oil pump in the desert."

"Yeah," Bdeniowitz nodded. "I didn't remember a boat up there."

"There's something else," Gleason added. "O'Shaunessey thought it was funny you wanted to know about a sailboat over the fireplace, because they found what was left of a painting of a sailboat *in* the fireplace."

Bdeniowitz turned to look at Gleason, then turned back to Windrow. Windrow screwed up his bruise and scratched where it met the corner of his eye. "That picture of the boat was *ARCADIA*, the *ARCADIA* II."

"Looks like somebody sank her," Gleason said gravely. "The frame and stretchers were broken up and the canvas was wrapped around them." He made a twisting motion with his hands. "The whole mess was laid in on top of some newspapers and woodscraps, partially burned."

"But it hadn't been completely burned?" Windrow asked.

Gleason shook his head. "Nope. O'Shaunessey said they could still make out most of the canvas when they spread it out. There's a sunset, a sailboat with two masts and the name on the boat was, ah..." He began to thumb through his spiral notebook.

"*ARCADIA II*," Bdeniowitz said. He looked at Windrow. "What's it mean, apple?"

Windrow shook his head. "Beats me, Max. When I got there the oil pump was on the way out, and the sailboat was on the wall. The kid told you that, right?"

"We didn't know to ask him about the paintings. But we'll check on it. Hell, I believe you. The thing is, what's this got to do with the Neil woman?"

Windrow was silent.

Gleason scratched his head. "I guess someone just didn't like her taste in art?" he ventured, and shrugged.

"Do you think it was the same type that doesn't like private detectives?" Bdeniowitz said.

Windrow looked at him. "You mean you believe that business about the limousine?"

Bdeniowitz scowled. "We found a black Cadillac limousine in the Presidio the day after they brought you in here. Front end was bashed in, the water was all gone out of the radiator, and the motor was locked up. There was paint and plastic from your Toyota all over the front end. There was a piece of your license plate embedded in the radiator core. So your end of the story checks out." Bdeniowitz paused. "More or less," he added.

Windrow frowned. "You found the car the day after they brought me in here?"

"Yeah."

"So what day is this? How long have I been in here?"

"They brought you in here on Tuesday. This is Thursday morning."

"So I've been in here two days?"

"Two days, Marty. More or less."

Two days, Windrow thought to himself. So, Jodie's been gone five. How long had she been in trouble? She'd called for help on Tuesday morning.

"So how come somebody wants you dead that close to the Neil murder?" Bdeniowitz persisted.

Anything could have happened, Windrow thought to himself. Everything could have happened. "I don't know," he said aloud. He threw the bedclothes to one side. His arm ached, but it worked. "Has anybody seen Woodruff?"

"Not a sign of him," Bdeniowitz said glumly. "What are you doing?"

"I'm getting out of here." He stood up. He heard a rush of surf in his ears and saw sparks when he closed his eyes. He steadied himself on the bedstand and knocked the empty glass off the table onto the floor. It bounced and spun to a standstill, unbroken.

"Hey," said Bdeniowitz, standing up.

"I'm all right," said Windrow. "Just excited about getting on the case for my client."

"You got a client? Who?

"Woodruff."

"Woodruff?"

Windrow breathed deeply and screwed his eye up so the bruise smarted. That gave him something to concentrate on. "Hand me my duds. I'm checking out of here."

Chapter Nine

MAD BRUCE KICKED A TIRE ON A 1964 FORD FAIRLANE.
"Listen," he said, "It's red, dearie, inside and out." He
shrugged. "So there's a little chrome missing." He waved.
"You can restore it on weekends." He pulled open the door
on the driver's side, and the sheet metal at the hinge jamb
popped. "Steering wheel, radio, dash pocket, ash tray, the
seats in fair shape..." He patted a thatch of duct tape on the
driver's seat. "Two visors, dome light." He flicked the switch
on the dome light back and forth, and shrugged. "Needs a
bulb." He pulled the seatback forward, revealing two empty
oil cans sitting on a nest of brown pine needles and yellowed
newspaper. "Plenty of room in back. You could practically
live in it, and you definitely," he winked lasciviously, "could
spend some time in it at the drive-in, my man my man."

Windrow looked under the hood. "Start it," he said. Mad
Bruce ground the starter and the motor caught. "Rev her
up," Windrow shouted. Mad Bruce floored the accelerator.
The four-barrel carburetor moaned, the V-8 roared under
it, the fan belt squealed. Blue smoke began to fill the car lot
behind the Ford. There didn't seem to be too much blowby,
judging by the breather on the valve cover, and the pollu-
tion equipment had already been added. He took the cap
off the radiator. The water was only about an inch low. "Turn
it off," he shouted. The motor continued to run wide open.

Windrow looked out from under the hood and drew a finger across his throat. Mad Bruce made a fist over his shoulder and let his eyes and head droop, like a hanged man. He opened one eye and looked at Windrow. Windrow looked at him. Mad Bruce raised his head and drew one forefinger rapidly in and out of his closed fist, grinning and jerking his eyebrows wildly. Windrow stared dully at him. Mad Bruce shrugged and killed the motor.

Windrow checked the brakes, the automatic transmission fluid, the lights, the dimmer switch, the turn signals, windshield wipers, and the tires. Everything he tested was legal. He slammed the hood and they took a drive. Mad Bruce tuned in a salsa disco station, loud, and made yipping noises along with the music.

The sun was out in the Mission District. Windrow let the red Ford loaf along under the palms of Dolores St. At the end of the block, pigeons circled the tower of Mission Dolores and the brakes did their job at the stop sign. Young girls in uniforms, just out of Catholic school, stood in groups in front of an ice cream store. Each clutched an armload of books, and wore a pleated skirt and knee socks, in brown or grey or navy blue, with matching sweaters and white blouses. Without exception, they all looked too big for their clothes.

Windrow turned down 16th street. A 1967 Impala with fender skirts, curb feelers, twinkling wheel covers and its rocker panels perhaps two inches off the ground came the other way. Its rear end suddenly leaped up with two discreet bounces and just as suddenly collapsed, until it seemed that its undercarriage must surely drag the ground. *En passant*, its radio was louder than the Fairlane's.

Mad Bruce leaned between Windrow and the steering wheel, honked the horn, and screamed at the Impala as it passed.

"Aieee hermanito! Arriba arriba abajo abajo. Low and slow del camino!" He leaned back and slapped Windrow on the arm. "Cruisin con la gente Martín, aieee!" He threw his head back and howled like a Bedouin woman in mourning. In his rear view mirror Windrow could see the Impala, stopped for the light at Dolores. The Impala's rear end raised and lowered, raised, raised some more, dropped again, like an insect deep into a mating ritual.

Mad Bruce adjusted his shades and grinned. "$595," he screamed over the blast of the radio.

Windrow drove and said nothing. At the intersection of 16th and Guerrero the light was red. He stopped. An early seventies model Pontiac, immaculately waxed, pulled up next to them. It contained a man and a woman. As they all waited for the light to change the Pontiac's front end slowly began to rise in the air, until the entire car was at about a fifteen degree angle to the street. Then its rear began to rise. The man and woman stared straight ahead. The man's teeth were clinched in a grin. His passenger was trying not to laugh, but the side of her face close to Windrow wrinkled and contorted. Her eyes stole a glance at Windrow and she blushed and giggled as she jerked them forward again. The front end of her car lowered a few inches and stopped. The back end lowered a few inches, stopped, then fell a foot. The woman was giggling. Abruptly, the front end dropped all the way to the street, and the rear end of the car shot back up. The woman could no longer control her laughing, and she slapped the driver on his shoulder, as if to make him stop. The front end of the car rose again in a series of coy increments. The woman hid her face in her hands. Her shoulders were shaking with laughter. The driver stared straight ahead and grinned sheepishly.

The light turned green. Windrow left them at the crosswalk, the Pontiac still jerking about, going nowhere.

"Awright," Mad Bruce said, squirming in his seat and looking out his window. "You're buying today, right? Cash? O.K. For you-today-only-right-now; E-Z terms; five seventy-five take it home."

Windrow said nothing. At the intersection the light was red. As he stopped he turned the radio down and looked at Mad Bruce. The Pontiac pulled up next to them. Mad Bruce looked at Windrow. Windrow turned and yelled to the driver of the Pontiac.

"Hey 'migo, how much you think this Ford is worth?"

The woman, closer to Windrow, looked at the driver. The driver slowly turned his head toward them and raised his sleepy eyebrows fractionally. He lifted his chin about one-half of an inch and surveyed the length of the Fairlane. A conversation ensued between the man and the woman in Caló undertones so rapid and full of slang that Windrow couldn't understand it. The light turned green. A car behind the Pontiac honked its horn. The driver of the Pontiac made a face and stroked his chin.

"Four hundred fifty simoleons, conquistadór," he said.

"Gracias," Windrow said. He turned right through the intersection. Mad Bruce protested loudly by yelling Caló imprecations past Windrow at the Pontiac as it disappeared behind them.

Windrow made a couple of turns and soon they found themselves on the South Van Ness on-ramp to 101. Once on the freeway, he pressed the accelerator. The speedometer wound easily to ninety. No doubt about it, the car had power, leg room and comfort, three things he'd missed in the Toyota. Bruised as he was, each trip to the grocery in the

Toyota would have been a hejira of endurance and discomfort; whereas now, in this red Ford, though a case should
pound him into the ground, he might ride from beating to
beating in style.

There was something satisfactory in that.

They drifted over the city, past the old Hamm's brewery
building, and merged onto 101 South, the road to San Jose,
and ultimately Los Angeles. The Ford was smooth. Neither
the front end or the recapped tires betrayed telltale vibrations at cruising speed.

He saw her as he was decelerating onto the army Street
off ramp.

Jodie Ryan was in the passenger seat of some kind of
station wagon, a Chevy, heading north. Her blonde hair, her
face, were unmistakable. Her features waxed golden among
the flat blur of concrete, metal and sun-faded automotive
enamels flowing up the other side of the freeway. Someone
wearing a ten gallon hat was driving her car; he hadn't time
to see who, but it could have been Sal. Could have been.

On the other hand, might not somebody with a ten gallon hat, short one Caddy, have switched to Chevrolet?

He pressed the accelerator, then braked and cursed. A
huge, slow-moving truck filled the lane marked Army Street
East. He guided the squealing car down and through the
maze of ramps that led to Army Street West. At the first intersection, he slid around the median—an illegal U turn—and
put the accelerator to the floor. Much to Windrow's purpose
the Fairlane leaped toward, though also sideways a little bit.
He flicked the wheel a couple of times as the car sloughed
east down under the freeway and up again, and regained
control of its forward motion in time to spin the wheel left,
snatch the emergency brake and slide around the median
again, another illegal U turn. The car wallowed sideways

across two lanes of oncoming traffic as it slid right, then left, then right again, and onto the northbound on-ramp. Again he put the gas pedal to the floor, and the little V-8 torqued the red car up the ramp and onto the Bay Shore again, now heading north at 75 mph.

Through all of this maneuvering, Mad Bruce, holding onto the dashboard with one hand and the armrest on the door with the other hand, yelling over the din of engine and tires, had begun to lower his price. He started with $560, clipped to $550 as they slid around the first median, went to $545 as they dropped under the overpass, feebly as if seasick mentioned $525 as they slid around the median for the second time, and finally, after shouting "OK OK OK charo, five hundred, five hundred dollars," gloomily retreated to four ninety-five after the armrest came off the door in his hand.

Windrow ignored him and accelerated up the hill as fast as the car would go. He weaved among cars across all five lanes until he gained a clear lane in the middle of the freeway. They hurtled past the Vermont St. exit, and topped the hill, where the vast network of the city spread below them. They could see all of downtown, the pyramid, the Bank of America building, Coit Tower beyond, they could see Marin County and the Bay Bridge. The freeway split in two at the bottom of the hill and there, Windrow thought, he saw the two-tone Wagonaire heading to the right, where 101 split onto Interstate 80, heading East. If so, the Fairlane was in the wrong lane.

The speedometer bouncing on ninety-five he swerved right across three lanes of traffic just in time to narrowly miss the impact-drums around which the freeway divided at the bottom of the hill. Distressed automobile horns sounded all around the wake of the red Ford, but he was gaining on the station wagon. Windrow adroitly maneuvered through the congestion to the right rear of the two-tone wagon. Its license plate read GUSH. The full head of blonde hair and the western-cut shirt in the passenger seat could have belonged to Jodie, but when he saw the tortoise shell hairpin, shaped like a big eighth-note, he knew it was her. Never would he allow more than this thirty feet of asphalt to come between him and her again.

The hood was drawing even with the rear of the wagon when the Ford ran out of gas.

At first Windrow didn't realize what had happened; he just knew the motor had died with the accelerator pressed all the way to the floor. Its momentum caused the Ford to hold even with the wagon, just for a second, before it began to fall back, and he pressed the hornring, hard.

It didn't work. He slammed the hornring with his fist, the entire mechanism sprang out of the steering wheel hub and into his lap. He cursed and yelled. He screamed out the window as the Ford began to slow and the wagon slowly pulled ahead. The blonde never turned around.

The hardest thing Windrow could remember having to do in a long time was resisting his urge to sideswipe the station wagon. The two cars were running side by side on a crowded freeway at sixty miles an hour. Cars were merging from a blind left ramp into the lane that contained the station wagon. Cars were all around them. To ram his Ford into the Chevy would be to invite disaster. Windrow gripped the wheel and cursed. He pumped the accelerator. Nothing. He glanced at the gas gauge. The needle rested in the unindexed void below Empty.

Seething with rage, he merged right and coasted down the off ramp of the Seventh St. exit. The light at its end was green, and he let the car roll across the intersection and down Bryant St., until it came to a stop. Windrow ground his teeth so hard he could taste shavings off his fillings. His knuckles glowed whitely along the rim of the red steering wheel. He angrily backhanded the hornring out of his lap. It was a gesture of impotence. Several little parts rolled around on the floor.

Mad Bruce huddled against the right hand door, clutching the severed armrest with both hands. He shook like he had yellow fever compounded by hypothermia.

"F-f-f-our h-h-hund-d-d... t-t-t-tw...," he said.

Windrow turned off the ignition switch. Putting the gear lever in park he glanced in the rear view mirror. The glass was full of alternating blue and red lights. He turned and looked out the back window. The colorful lights were on the roof of a California Highway Patrol car.

To his left, out the window, wide gray steps rose between green hedges to a row of glass doors that opened into a building he knew only too well. The red Ford had come to a stop in the six hundred block of Bryant Street, directly in front of San Francisco Police Headquarters.

Windrow turned and looked at Mad Bruce.

"Sold," he said.

Chapter Ten

"LOOK, APPLE. I'M NOT RESPONSIBLE FOR YOUR ECCEN-tricities on the highway. You got a private ticket? So what? It doesn't give you license to drive sideways on the Bay Shore. Only cops can get away with that and, lest you forget, you are not a cop no more, ever."

"Max," said Windrow patiently, "I'm telling you. It was Jodie Ryan in a late model Chevy Wagonaire. The goddam license plate said GUSH. A ten gallon hat was driving. A ten gallon hat tried to kill me with a Cadillac. The Ryan girl has these two tortoise shell hairpins; they're shaped like musical notes; I saw one on this blonde's head... It had to be her..."

Bdeniowitz slammed his fist on his desk, his face red-dened. "So what? All she did was stand you up. As far as we're concerned, she's done nothing. Nothing! Sure we'd like to talk to her. But there's no evidence connecting her with this Neil case. Sure there's a lot of ten gallon hats in this. Are you telling me that's a lead? I mean, you got *one hard fact*?"

Bdeniowitz didn't expect an answer. He drummed his fingers on his desk and smoldered. The highway patrol-man, who had finally allowed Windrow to convince him to come upstairs and talk to the chief of homicide, cleared his throat. His aviation sunglasses made his visage opaque, but his intent was clear. That Windrow might be on a case mol-

lified the CHP's view of the incident to a certain extent, but
Mad Bruce's dealer plates were out of date, there had been
two phone calls to the CHP from terrified motorists. Windrow had in fact broken several laws, and the CHP, being a
tidy outfit, would like to write these two clowns up for these
things. Bdeniowitz waved his hand at the patrolman.

"Throw the book at him," he growled. The telephone at
his elbow whimpered. "Wait a minute." He picked up the
receiver. "What," he barked.

Seated next to Windrow, Mad Bruce whined and fidg-
eted. Windrow squinted. The fluorescent light buzzed on
the ceiling. Through the window behind Bdeniowitz, Windrow could see the tops of several eastbound trucks stalled
on the freeway. They inched forward, they stopped, they
inched forward some more. He mused on the irony of the
coincidence. Either the stalled traffic was less than twenty
minutes late, or he and the Chevy Wagonaire had arrived
twenty minutes early. Had they encountered this snarl he
might have walked up to Jodie's window, tapped on it with a
fingernail and politely asked her what the hell was going on,
and what sort of trouble would she be in exactly?

But already the previous coincidence had seemed, after
all, a great deal to ask of the huge number of possibilities available. Spotting the Ryan girl on the freeway? Ridiculous. But
running out of gas had evened that one out, alright. Coincid-
ing with a traffic jam would have been too much. Having the
links of fate and randomness shape a chain of events like that,
a man could just sit back and let things happen. But they'd
missed the traffic jam, and the Ford had run out of gas, and
the Chevy wagon was gone. It was like two boats separated
and helplessly tossed in the unheeding surf of random events;
in spite of all the rowing anyone might do, at one moment the

boats are separated, the next they're about to crash into each other, then they lose sight of one another completely.

Windrow ground his teeth. You don't get a chance like that every day, and the appearance of one lucky shot made it even more unlikely another would turn up. Still, he'd nearly turned it to his advantage. Oddly enough, without the Ford he would not have been able to so much as make the attempt. The Toyota would have been incapable of a chase like that. The Toyota had never been able to get out of third gear on that particular grade above Army street. He looked at the check Mad Bruce held in his hand and idly wondered if he would be able to cover it. In any case, Windrow decided, he was going to like this Ford, it would give him a new edge on coincidence.

Bdeniowitz got off the phone.

"GUSH is registered to the O'Ryan Petroleum Co., care of a P.O. Box in Taft, California," he said.

"Do tell."

Bdeniowitz scowled. "I don't have to tell you a damn thing, apple."

"You need to be looking for another cowgirl in this case, Max," Windrow said. "Dresses like a high priced cowboy: ten gallon hat, suit, fancy boots, packs a gun and rolls of quarters. Goes by the name of Sal, acts like a man, but he's a she."

Bdeniowitz raised an eyebrow. The highway patrolman cleared his throat. Windrow gestured at him. "Now can we put out an APB?"

"You're the one broke the law," the highway patrolman observed softly.

Windrow rolled his eyes, tapped his foot four times, and sighed loudly.

"For what?" Bdeniowitz said. "APB for what? What're the charges?"

Windrow shrugged. "Murder one?"

"There's not a shred of—." The phone interrupted Bdeniowitz. He picked up the receiver and shouted, "What?!"

Windrow felt a damp hand on his arm.

"I want mi madre," Mad Bruce whimpered. "Madre mía." Windrow looked at him and noticed for the first time that Mad Bruce's eyes were tremendously dilated. "She got me into this," Mad Bruce said distractedly, addressing a point on Windrow's shoulder. The check slipped from Mad Bruce's fingers and fluttered to the floor. Windrow pursed his lips: it didn't bounce.

The highway patrol cleared his throat politely. "You dropped your check, sir."

Mad Bruce smiled faintly. "Sir," he said, with a trace of wonder in his voice. "He called me Sir...."

Bdeniowitz hung up the telephone. His face was changed. He arched an eyebrow as made a few notes on a yellow legal pad. Then he picked up the telephone again and pushed a button.

"Gleason. I want an APB out for a Miss Jodie Ryan. Yeah. That's the one. Last seen about an hour ago, on Interstate 80 just beyond the Seventh St. exit, heading East. Late model Chevy Wagonaire, two-tone white on grey, Cal license plate Gamma Uptown Sigma Howdy.... Hang on," he looked at Windrow, "Windrow has the make." He extended the telephone receiver across the desk toward Windrow and looked him in the eye.

Windrow balked. He'd wanted to find Jodie Ryan, and the police could help him do it, but something had changed. Now they had reasons of their own for finding her.

"What's up?" he asked.

Bdeniowitz wagged the phone once at him.

Windrow took the telephone. "Steve?"

Gleason's voice came from the other end.

"Hey yuh hey yuh, it's Fireball Windrow hisself. He's a comin' round the third turn and he's neck and neck with— what's this? The California Highway Patrol, folks! It's a Plymouth and a Ford, folks, fender to fender. MoPar and FoMoCo. Fireball cuts in the afterburner and scorches a trench in the blacktop. The CHP fingers the stud that fires the photon speeding citation. He—"

"Blonde," said Windrow, "she's a blonde. Twenty-eight years old, about five-eight, one-fifteen, green eyes, plays music for a living. She's got an agent, name of Lobe..."

"Lobe," said Gleason on the phone.

"Lobe?" said Bdeniowitz.

"Hooker, eh?" said Gleason

"Poor kid," said Bdeniowitz.

"And her granddaddy was Sweet Jesus O'Ryan, the oilman. Recently deceased."

Windrow hung up the phone.

"What happened, Max? Why the sudden help?"

"We got some hard evidence," Bdeniowitz smiled. "The lab matched a dent in the Neil woman's skull with a corner on that broken guitar neck."

Mad Bruce shuddered and his teeth chattered. He hugged himself and rocked in his chair.

Windrow shrugged. "Yeah, well we all knew that the splinters matched, too. But the instrument was wiped clean, right?"

Bdeniowitz smiled larger. "Yes, it was. But on one end of this guitar neck there is this little screw-on plate that covers a gadget you adjust the neck with."

"The truss rod," the highway patrolman interjected politely. Windrow and Bdeniowitz looked at him. The patrolman stood just as he'd been standing since they'd arrived at Bdeniowitz's office, erect, hands clasped behind his back, feet spread slightly apart. At ease.

"The plate's on the peghead, right above the nut," he added helpfully.

"Yeah," said Bdeniowitz. "So anyway, somebody downstairs thought to unscrew this little plate and check the back of it for prints. They found a perfect thumb, left hand. It mates with the left hand of one Jodie O'Ryan. She managed a DUI about nine or ten years ago in Bakersfield."

"Right. That was before she dropped the O from her name. Nice work. But that just means she'd had her hands on the guitar once. She might own it—seems likely any guitar around that house would be hers—but it doesn't mean she killed anybody with it. I mean, you don't think she adjusted the truss rod just in order to kill somebody with the thing.... Do you?"

Bdeniowitz nodded. "No. But it's a fact. It gives us a reason to go looking for her, and that might turn up something else."

Windrow frowned. He stood up and paced a circle.

"What's the matter, apple? It's what you wanted, isn't it?"

"Not exactly," Windrow muttered.

Bdeniowitz sighed. "Well here's another curveball for you."

"What," said Windrow, only half listening, still pacing.

"You'll recall the Neil woman had sex before she was dumped over the cliff."

Windrow thought about it for a minute, but said nothing.

"It was a little bit rough," Bdeniowitz added, quietly. "More like assault. She was... torn up."

Windrow stopped pacing. "Wouldn't that indicate a man...?"

Bdeniowitz chewed his lip and shook his head. "Mere brutality. There's no direct evidence one way or the other. No semen, no hair, but assault to the sexual parts." Bdeniowitz cleared his throat. He was obviously uncomfortable, and that annoyed him. "Forced penetration, perpetrated before death." He spoke quietly. "They can't say what did the penetrating, just yet."

Windrow hissed. "Jesus."

Mad Bruce breathed deeply and noisily. He clutched Windrow's arm. Windrow saw that Mad Bruce had turned a bad shade of gray.

"One more thing."

"Now what?"

"Mrs. Neil wasn't Mrs. Neil when she died. She married a guy called," he read from his notepad, "Thurman Woodruff, in Las Vegas, on Monday last."

Windrow raised an eyebrow.

"The day of O'Ryan's funeral." "You find him yet? You talked to him?"

Bdeniowitz shook his head. "Gallery's closed. No sign of Woodruff. Little card in the window says, 'By Appointment Only.' Antique dealer next door says that's brand-new policy, since about Tuesday, and nobody's been around since the card appeared. We're looking for him."

"Funny he should disappear like that," Windrow mused. "He's in line for a lot of dough." He shook his head. He had a feeling, as if there were ants crawling up his sternum. "Don't know. It would seem like Pamela Neil's health wouldn't be his most pressing interest, but on the other hand it could be ok—if he's in the clear."

"Could be the guy's stiff himself."

"You think?"

Bdeniowitz made a face. "Why think when there's all this action to watch?" he grumbled. "The way things are going, pretty soon there won't be any principals left. Either way, apple, there's big money swamping these people. Anything could happen. People die every day for a lot less." Bdeniowitz twirled his chair so that he faced the freeway, his back to the room.

"Gilbert," said Bdeniowitz, after a pause.

"Yessir," said the highway patrolman.

"I don't think we need to press charges on these gentlemen. It would seem that they might actually have been in the process of attempting to perform a public service when you apprehended them. Expunge the record, or something."

"Yessir," said Gilbert.

"If there's any problem, have your office call my office."

"Yessir."

"You got anything to add, apple?"

Windrow helped Mad Bruce to his feet. The man looked terrible. "Nothing," said Windrow.

Bdeniowitz didn't turn around. "Keep in touch," he muttered.

Windrow retrieved his check from the floor and led Mad Bruce through the door.

On the street, the highway patrolman took a can out of the trunk of the CHP car and put a gallon of gas into the red Fairlane, while Mad Bruce threw up behind the pyrochanthus next to the front steps of the police station. Windrow leaned against the fender of the Ford with his hands in his pockets and watched the fill up. After a while, he asked Officer Gilbert if he played music.

Officer Gilbert grinned over the gas can. "Every Friday

and Saturday night. Lounge in Walnut Creek called the Flank and Tankard." He pulled the filler spout out of the gas tank and screwed the cap on.

"Really," said Windrow. "What sort of music?"

"C & W mostly, some pop stuff."

"Ever heard of Jodie Ryan?"

"Sure," said Gilbert. "We do a tune of hers called "Stealin' Eyes." You know it?"

Windrow squinted his sore peeper. "Fancy that. Ever meet her?"

"No sir, never have." Gilbert let the hinged license plate snap back over the gas cap and stood up. "She's a real talent, she is."

"Yeah," said Windrow. He scratched the bruised crow's foot behind his eye. Gilbert said goodbye and left. A few minutes later Mad Bruce limped out of the bushes. His voice was weak, but his complexion was much healthier, more like its natural pasty white color. They got in the Ford.

"Jesus," Mad Bruce said. He leaned back against the seat and exhaled loudly. As Windrow ground the starter, he glanced at the empty plastic bag. It was under the severed armrest between Mad Bruce's feet.

"How much did you eat?" he said. The motor caught once and died.

"Oh, compadre," Mad Bruce groaned. "I ate the whole fuckin' stash. I had sopors, like, you know, a couple quaaludes and some valiums..."

The motor caught. Windrow revved it a couple of times. Blue smoke filled the rear-view mirror. He pulled the column lever into drive and eased the Ford into the sporadic traffic on Bryant Street, to his right.

"...and some cross-tops, man," Mad Bruce continued, counting on his fingers and shaking his head, "yeah, fuckin' good cross-tops and I think some yellow jackets, and some of that gooood colombo man, two or three joints, and goddamit, there was a couple *poppers* in there Martín..." He looked at Windrow with wide eyes and an appalled, open mouth. "You ever *eat* amyl nitrite, man?" He belched loudly and covered his mouth. "Oh, hombre don't let get around no open flame...."

Chapter Eleven

"S'WHAT, S'WHAT AREADY?"

The two inch speaker in the intercom made Harry Lobe's gravelly voice sound worse than usual. Beer trucks and buses lumbered up and down the lower Turk Street, their fumes mixed with the stench of Lysol that wafted from the peep show next door. Old newspapers huddled against the vertical bars that completely covered the entrance to Lobe's building, but the mesh couldn't keep out the urine and spit and any other fluid ephemera that cared to penetrate it enough to stain the walls and steps beyond.

Sister Opium Jade's husky tones got huskier.

"Harry?" she pleaded. "Harry, I'm sick Harry."

The speaker circuit clicked back to send and they could hear the claustrophobic ambiance of Lobe's ten by ten office. His desk chair squeaked.

"What: you a comic?" The speaker clicked.

"Harry," she pleaded, moving with her body and voice at the speaker as if it were a sailor in a dance hall. "Harry, I need work."

"Who is this?"

Sister Opium Jade rolled her eyes at Windrow and cooed, "Mary Simms, Harry. Cooka sent me. She said you could get me some work. I need work, Harry. I'm good but I'm sick, Harry."

Another pause. They could hear that the speaker was still in its microphonic mode, listening to the street. Opium Jade leaned until her ruby lacquered lips were not an inch from the filthy grill, a perishable delicacy perilously close to imminent corrosion.

"The first one's free, Harry." She caressed the words so that they oozed through the little punctures in the dented metal.

The lock on the iron gate buzzed, and Windrow pushed it open.

Lobe's office was in the top of the building in the back. It should have been a closet, but Lobe had the rest of the building rented out to the faded list of faceless enterprises listed on a piece of plywood wired behind the grate above the doorbells. The peep show would appear to be the only legitimate business on the premises, so long as you didn't look too hard into the system of mirrors that owned it.

But Windrow didn't give a damn about that. He took the steps three at a time, to spite his soreness. When he got to the top he stood there, shaking. The anticipation worked the valves and circuits in him, uncoiling the wounded animal. For the first time in a week adrenaline laced him with its unique favor, united all the quirks and bruises of his system for him. He pushed Lobe's office door until it banged flat against the wall, to the left behind it.

Lobe's desk faced the hall, with room for the door to clear and then some. He was sitting behind it. Eight by ten glossy photographs, nude, obscene and otherwise, some personalized, mostly yellowed and curled, covered the peeling green walls above a battered wainscot. There were a couple of file cabinets to the left, another chair beneath a grimy window to the right.

Lobe was a fat hairless man with a round greenish-yellow face that looked like the bottom of a gallon jug of cheap chablis held up to a street light. His cranial features concealed a small handful of hydrated dolomite that passed for brains but could have passed for the same yellowish gluten that passed for his flesh that for all the world looked like it would present the same unvarying consistency to the thoughtful bullet passing through its center from any direction. Like, for example, in one ear and out the other.

Lobe, for his part, had a pretty low opinion of Windrow. Had he known who had come buzzing his buzzer this a.m. Lobe wouldn't have granted admittance if only to provide Windrow some minor irritation. Lobe saw Windrow as a cipher equal to zero in his nickel abacus: no more, no less. Windrow's permanent absence from Lobe's sordid scene seemed like an okay idea to Lobe, his presence a nuisance.

Under normal circumstances, in either case, there was no way Lobe thought Windrow worth the sweat of gunplay. But today circumstances must have been waxing abnormal. Lobe was expecting trouble. To cope, he was keeping, a revolver handy in the partially opened desk drawer over his lap. Whereas, Sister Opium Jade's voice coming over the speaker box on his desk had been an unexpected relief to him, the appearance of Windrow's gangly and distinctly unfeminine frame in the doorway surprised Lobe badly. But, as Windrow deduced from the information-giving and-receiving tics of Lobe's eyes—the *saccadic* eye movements, the ones directly related to thinking or, as in Lobe's case, to the manipulation of small potatoes that passed for thinking—his appearance was not the surprise Lobe was expecting to be surprised by.

All this Windrow took in at a glance, it used up only a second. Then he got his own surprise.

It was a pleasant one.

Lobe went for the blaster anyway.

Lobe hadn't intended to pull a gun on Windrow; he had it handy for somebody else. Windrow suspected the discrepancy. Having gone for the piece in his initial moment of surprise, Lobe hesitated when he saw it was Windrow, the wrong party. But then, he saw that Windrow was going to act adversely, a counter move, and his mind restarted the reflexes it had just called off: he thought to pull the gun out just to cover himself. And, while he was at it, maybe he would shoot this jerk Windrow anyway. Self-defense against a trespasser. All this decision-making took time. It took, maybe, a quarter of a second.

That little bit of time allowed Windrow to savor a foretaste of the immense pleasure he was about to get out of legitimately preventing himself from being shot. He grinned hugely, and saw the slow dawn of terror in Lobe's previously business-like eyes. He raise his right leg, placed the ball of his shoe against the edge of Lobe's desk, and kicked, hard.

Though plenty big, the desk was cheap and light; it slid easily. Lobe's swivel chair rolled backwards a few inches to the wall, the drawer pushed against his huge stomach and closed on his hand. The gun discharged in the drawer, blowing a large hole in the side of the desk. The slug struck the wastebasket to Windrow's right. It clanked dully. Further pressure to the desk meanwhile pushed the air out of Lobe and into the room with a great whoosh. As a byproduct of its motion the gasp made a sort of yell as its air passed Lobe's vocal chords, but the sound of it was lost in Windrow's ape-like roar.

Windrow turned loose of the doorframe and leaned over the desk. He grabbed Lobe by the roll of fat that bulged over the leading edge of the desk with his right hand and the knot of his tie with his left. Turning as he pulled, he lifted the big man out of his chair over the desk and launched him over his hip, back toward the hallway. The desk turned over against Windrow's leg as he made this move, and the motion caught Lobe's wrist between the drawerface and the edge of the desk. The hand came out of the drawer all right, but not before the wrist snapped and a wide stripe of skin peeled back from the wristbone to the second knuckle on the thumb and forefinger. Lobe gulped the stale air of the office and howled.

But, as he turned and released the fat agent, Windrow saw too late that, having banged against its hinge wall when opened, the door had drifted back on its return arc, nearly closing again. So that Lobe, flying out of Windrow's grasp, crashed through the cheap panels of the door and into the hall beyond.

Windrow couldn't help but laugh at Lobe's misfortune, a short bark of a laugh, and with the laugh about half of his animosity toward the big man went out of him. So he paused the mayhem. Now maybe Lobe would talk to him. He was about to pull open the shattered rectangle of splinters that had been the door and drag the poor sap back inside, let bygones be bygones, when, with an animal roar, Lobe exploded through the calendar that still somehow hung over the splinters. He was wielding a short piece of wood, like a club.

So this is how you make it in show business, Windrow thought: Perseverance. He stood his ground and unloaded his right fist from the back wall into Lobe's face at arm's length—you never give up, he thought. Lobe's head stopped dead in the air and the rest of him folded around it and went past and he dropped to the floor, flat on his back, with a crash. The piece of board hit Windrow lightly in the shin.

Sister Opium Jade struck a pose in the door and inhaled a low whistle through her pursed lips.

"He'd a crushed me to death," she observed. She looked

at Windrow admiringly. "Mah hero. You has done saved me from a grisly squash-job."

"We're even, babe," said Windrow, shaking out his fingers. "I can't tell you how good that felt."

"I knows sumpin what feels mo better..."

"Can the Uncle Remus and see if you can find some water."

He uprighted the desk, leaving the spilled trash on the floor. He leaned Lobe against the front of it. He got the gun out of the drawer and unloaded it. Then he took the time to quickly shake down the office. He pulled open file drawers until he found a folder marked Ryan, J. He opened it and stopped. The first item in the folder was an 8×10 of Jodie Ryan's face, which he'd seen before. He had a copy in his own office. He liked it. He dropped the slugs from the pistol into the file drawer and closed it.

Opium Jade returned with a little paper cup full of water and looked over Windrow's shoulder.

"Country," she said. "Bread and butter and milk and eggs and dewsilky moo-cows in the misty upper forty—at $10,000 an acre, of course."

Windrow grunted.

"And if you believe that," she added, "you're a sap and I'll give you a license that says so."

"I already have a license."

"Not to drive that rig." She posed cutely with the dixie cup. "What do you want me to do with this?"

"Throw it in his face."

She poured it. Two ounces of water barely wet the vast surface that contained Lobe's salient features, but the big man moaned at the change.

Windrow laid the file on the desk and bent over the agent.

"Lobe. Can you hear me, Lobe?"

Lobe groaned and moved his head. Rivulets of water thinned the blood beaded along the seams of a dozen scratches on his face. It looked like glacial melt running off Half Dome in a red sunset.

"Why the heavy play, Lobe? You forget how to talk with your hands full?"

Lobe moved his lips. Sounds came out, none of them English.

Windrow furrowed his brow. "What's he saying?"

"Fuck you, I think," Opium Jade surmised.

"Off." Lobe managed to open his mouth long enough to form the O. "Fuck... off."

"I'm surprised at you, Lobe. You don't want to fry for shooting lil ol us. Who were you staying ready for?"

Lobe moved his head from side to side with his eyes squeezed shut. The fat bunching around his stubby black lashes, the only hair on his head, made them look like two nasty stitched-up wounds.

"Does it have anything to do with the Ryan girl?"

Lobe said nothing.

Windrow crouched close to the agent's swollen face and scowled. "Look, Lobe. We've gone this far, I don't mind taking the rest of the route. Do I have to maybe pull your tongue out a couple inches with a pair of pliers and hold matches under it?"

Opium Jade laughed, a high lilting chuckle that was spontaneous, but it had something decidedly anticipatory about it.

"Or maybe..."

Lobe's head began to sag to one side.

"He's fainted," Opium Jade said. "You scared him unconscious."

Windrow patted Lobe's vast jowls. They hung from both

sides of his face like dead meat in shallow water. "Lobe. Wake up!"

Lobe's head came back upright and the eyes became slits. Windrow could see the glint of the moisture in them. And he could see something else. Half conscious and his defenses down, Lobe's eyes showed one thing.

Lobe was scared.

Windrow frowned. "I didn't come here to kill you, Lobe. I came here to ask a couple of stupid questions. Some yes-no stuff. Maybe an address or two. Real simple."

Lobe's breath, shallow and slow when he was out, was gradually coming in short gasps. "I ain't scared of trash like you Windrow," he muttered. He arranged him back more or less vertically agains the desk and seemed to regain a bit of his oily composure. He pushed Windrow away. "I ain't scared of no washed-up Sears-Roebuck floorwalker."

"That's the spirit, kid. All I can do is strain you through the cracks in your floorboards. So why the piece?"

Lobe touched the corners of his mouth with the back of his ruined hand. He winced at the gesture, looked at his hand and the blood that came away with it. His eyes focused and he snarled. "None of your goddam business." He flailed his hands in front of him in an effort to overcome the elemental forces that held him to the floor. He teetered to the right and put out his hand to stop himself from falling over. The fingers barely touched the floor before he let out a yell and jerked his hand back so that he fell over. He clutched the mangled appendage to his chest and curled around it, cursing and grimacing.

"Yeah," said Windrow, standing up. "It's all my fault."

Lobe got to his feet, still clutching the bad hand to his chest, his face red with abrasions and rage. Windrow found a spark of admiration in himself for this fat chiseler. The guy had some guts in him.

Lobe began feebly to move his desk by pushing against it with his thigh, edging a corner of it out from the wall to get to his chair. Ignoring the scattered papers he bent to put the telephone back on the desk and replaced the receiver in its cradle.

Windrow stood up. "The Ryan girl," he said.

Having cleared enough space, Lobe uprighted the swivel chair and collapsed into it. He gripped the bad hand and sighed. Then the eyes opened and looked with undisguised hatred at Windrow.

"You should feel what that fluff does for the Lobe," he sneered.

Opium Jade let a small gasp escape her lips. She looked at Windrow. Windrow looked at Lobe. Three seconds ticked past. Then Windrow suddenly reached over the desk. He closed his big hand over Lobe's broken hand and squeezed. The blood started from the split skin over Windrow's knuckles.

Lobe screamed.

Windrow twisted.

Lobe pounded and chopped at Windrow's arm with his good hand but that made it hurt worse, and he howled.

"Awright, awright," he yelled.

Windrow twisted the other way. He hissed like a snake.

Lobe begged. Involuntary tears coursed his cheeks.

Windrow turned loose.

Lobe cuddled his ruined paw against his chest. The features of his face compressed into the smallest area possible, a focus of torment.

A minute passed, and another, before Lobe spoke.

"Ch-check out her ex," he gasped. "He's a studio talent called Roy Staple. Used to back her with his band. When she got some notice she dumped them both. He's been no good ever since. *Now get the fuck outta here!*"

Windrow could see that the pain was beginning to use up most of Lobe's willpower. "What about the other?" he said.

"What other?" Lobe hissed.

"Who's got you packing a gun?"

Lobe opened his eyes and looked at Windrow, measured him. Sweat beaded his forehead.

"Just some psychopath." He closed his eyes again. "Business is full of them Nothing I can't handle. Now get out of here, man. I gotta put in a call to Oral Roberts."

Windrow retrieved the manilla folder from the floor. The satisfaction he'd gotten out of mauling Lobe had somehow dissipated. There was more to Lobe than just the conniving agent he'd spoken with a half dozen times on the phone, and more to Lobe than the one-sided contract Jodie had shown him. He found himself inexplicably moved by an urge to help the fat man he'd rendered nearly helpless. He tapped the folder against his leg. The sound seemed to add to the silence in the office.

"Lobe. You want help?"

Lobe snorted. His features contorted from a grimace to a laugh and back again.

"You can't even help yourself, Windrow," he said. "How the hell can you do anything for me?"

"Tell me where the Ryan girl is."

"No idea. You got the only lead I'm hip to."

"Who's got you scared?"

Lobe said nothing.

"Look, Lobe. They could be the same people I'm after. Somebody made a try for me the day before yesterday. It wasn't professional, but it was vicious. They missed and I'm lucky to be walking around. The Ryan girl's stepmother was definitely bumped off, her stepfather is missing, the girl is missing, and grandpa is dead. Grandpa left enough money to buy Big Sur and build a glass dome over it. With Pamela Neil dead it probably all goes to Jodie. There's a sadistic clothes horse running around dressed like a cattle baron beating people up, very remote control and mysterious. I'd like to do something about it. If you know anything you should tell me. I don't know why they should care, whoever they are, but they might be the same people putting the heat on you. How do I know? Now I'm asking you one more time: Are you part of this or not?"

Lobe's expression had changed while Windrow was talking. "Jodie Ryan doesn't have a stepfather," he said.

"She does now. Three days after Grandpa died, they cremated him in Vegas. The ex-Mrs. Sweet Jesus O'Ryan got hitched to Thurman Woodruff, art dealer, about an hour later. They probably did it in the same chapel as the cremation, with the same congregation, for all I know. Now Mrs. Thurman Woodruff is an ex, period, and Mr. Thurman Woodruff's personal finances are no longer vague. That's if he's alive and if he's in the clear."

Lobe suddenly looked thoughtful, as if he'd forgotten all about his pain. Windrow thought that must involve some pretty interesting thinking.

Then Lobe snapped out of it and laid the telephone receiver on the desk in front of him. It was a rotary phone. He dialed seven digits and paused.

"Beat it Windrow, and take your whore with you."

"*Merde*." said Opium Jade.

"Cunt." Lobe spit the word.

Windrow looked at Lobe for a long moment. "Thanks, Lobe," he said evenly. "I was beginning to forget I don't like you." He held up the manilla folder. "I'm taking this with me. If you live long enough, I'll mail it back."

Lobe waited, saying nothing. Windrow could see he was gritting his teeth against the pain. "Don't count the Lobe out, dick," he said quietly, through clenched teeth. Even so, Windrow could hear the mean determination in the man's voice. Lobe had some guts, it was true, but it was his mean streak that kept him going, the same facet of his personality that allowed him to live off a stable of women. In any case, Lobe's meanness helped his personality like phlebotomy helped the plague.

Windrow pulled the pistol from his belt and laid it on top of the file cabinet. "If whoever it was caught up with me and the Neil dame catches up with you, Lobe, this gun isn't going to help."

Lobe scowled.

"Leave," he said.

Windrow held Opium Jade's hand while she picked her way through the pieces of door that littered the floor. In spite of her care, one of the spiked heels speared a piece of veneer. She held Windrow's shoulder with one hand while she cocked the leg straight back and pulled the shoe off. She had a nice leg and a pretty foot. Big. Smooth. The heel was calloused.

While she held the shoe, Windrow pulled the thin sheet of luan off it.

"Just like the old neighborhood," she said, replacing the shoe. She took the piece of wood out of Windrow's hand and tossed it back into the office behind them. It fluttered to the floor in front of Lobe's desk. "*Merde* all over the place."

As they came to the stairhead, Windrow heard Lobe dial the last digit.

He thought it might have been a zero.

Chapter Twelve

WINDROW AND SISTER OPIUM JADE WALKED TOGETHER down Market street, 3 blocks from Lobe's office. The sun brightened the air that blustered cool around them, full of gum wrappers and pigeons. They entered the tableau of poverty and addiction that spills out of the mouth of Sixth Street onto Market, so carefully displayed on the new bricks under the restored streetlamps. While they waited for the light, they watched a man on the other side of Sixth who stood with a frozen expression, moving his hands back and forth in front of his face as if he were climbing an invisible rope. He would climb for a while, hand over hand, then stop and plait invisible strands, top to bottom, neck to waist. Then he'd give the rope a stout tug, as if to snug up his work, and begin to climb again.

Across the sidewalk from the rope climber, a man wearing a sandwich board completely covered with tiny red and black writing waved a Bible and orated invective. Next to him, a young man with matted hair and a vacant stare strummed a ruined Spanish guitar with three strings and sang the one line 'bringing in the sheep' over and over. Not 'sheaves.' 'Sheep.'

The light changed. Office workers, bike messengers, businessmen, bums and tourists thronged between the stationary attractions. Two trolley cars released their brakes, rang their bells and rolled in opposite directions, each as if it were plumetting helplessly downhill. Sister Opium Jade slipped her arm through Windrow's and eyed the street corner characters.

"Pour peu que tu te bouges," she whispered, clinging to Windrow. "Renaissent tous mes désespoirs. And how."

"Honey," Windrow drawled sincerely, "I can't tell if you're ordering frog legs or snails, but we can't afford either one."

"I got enough for two, baby," Opium Jade said warmly, squeezing his elbow into the curve above her thinly sheathed hip. "Nothing but Willies up and down this street," she added.

"No Johns?"

She gave his hip a bump with hers, nearly knocking him over. "I already got one a them," she said huskily.

"You're barking up the wrong eucalyptus," Windrow said softly.

Opium Jade pouted. "Aw, Marty. Just one little kiss?" She bumped him again and winked. "On the cheek?"

Windrow smiled and cleared his throat. "I'm on a case," he said sternly. He shot his cuffs. "Best to keep my mind between my ears."

Opium Jade looked sideways at him. "Is that where you keep her? In your mind?" Her tone caught between teasing and serious.

Windrow looked at her. Their eyes met. Hers were big, almond shaped, with brown, almost black irises.

"Cause that's the only place you're going to keep her," she said quietly.

A drunk teetered into Windrow and exhaled the pheromones of a terminal corruption into his face. Windrow gently but firmly brushed the man away without taking his eyes off Opium Jade's.

The drunk stumbled a couple of feet, embraced a newspaper box and toppled over with it. Several people on the sidewalk gave Windrow stern glances and a wider berth.

He ignored them. "You're telling it," he said to Opium Jade.

"You want her too bad," she said simply. "It's affecting your judgement. I thought you were going to rip Lobe's arm off for making that cheap crack about her. Did you think that was chivalrous, or something?"

Windrow rolled his eyes. "It wasn't chivalry, it was fun."

Opium Jade made a face. "It was weakness, Marty. Lobe saw it before I did. He saw your throat and jabbed at it. With him it's instinctive. He's an unctuous fat pimp, but that just makes him better at cheap shots. You should have seen your face." She touched his arm. "No, I thought you were going to kill him for it."

A bus roared away from the curb beside them, making talk temporarily impossible. A man ran alongside banging on it and screaming curses. After a hundred feet or so the bus outran him and he gave up, walked to the curb and furiously kicked the back of a news kiosk. An old, grizzled newsie stuck his head out the front and looked around the side, but said nothing.

"She needs help," Windrow said. "She asked me for it."

"I don't know anything about that," Opium Jade said, shaking her head, "but I might be able to rope it into my theory later."

Windrow looked at her and smiled. She frowned.

"Look, Marty. It's none of my business, but what's a slick item like Jodie Ryan doing with a fuck-up like you?" She held up her hand. "Don't tell me: you're good in the sack?"

Windrow shrugged modestly. Opium Jade nodded.

"Okay, you're good in the sack. Here's a woman's got a record out, maybe a hit tune on it, and talent to back them up with. On top of that, her granddaddy just died and left her Southern California. Five years ago—if she was walking then—she needed an agent. She signed on with Lobe. She won't whore for him, but she hits the hay with Lobe once in a while to keep him happy."

Windrow bristled and stopped. "I don't buy that."

"Even if it's so he'll do what he can for her?" She shrugged. "So maybe she doesn't. Either way, he gets her exposure and keeps her working. That's good. After all, she's trying to make it in show business."

Windrow buried his hands in his pockets and watched his feet as they took their turns in front of him on the sidewalk. He didn't like what he was hearing, but he listened.

"But now she's just about used Lobe up. Like, she could probably sing the same song at the Grand Old Oprey every Christmas from now until the end of her life. Ain't that what it's about?" Opium Jade twirled a finger. "Anyway, the point is, she doesn't need Lobe anymore. His connections get her into a truckstop casino in Stateline, Nevada, on any Tuesday night—maybe—but no more. He couldn't do a television deal if his life depended on it, all the sharks in that game are five or six times bigger than he is. Not only that, he's a pimp. Nobody legitimate would even let him into the elevator."

"So the deal is," Windrow interrupted her, "scare Lobe so bad he'll simply do nothing until her contract expires. Or until he sells out."

"Right. But the kicker is, Jodie Ryan herself has the heaviest motive for wanting that to happen. Right?"

They heard a distant explosion. Opium Jade looked

behind them. Windrow, in midthought, paid no attention. A few of the people milling around them looked to one side or another as they hurried along the sidewalk, but no one gave any indication of seeing anything. An old man with white hair and a nicotine-stained beard looked up and held out his hands, palms up, muttering to himself. No fiery debris or chunks of concrete rained out of the sky onto his hands. The old man shrugged and clasped his hands, one over the other in front of him. He resumed pacing an obscure pattern of little steps back and forth on one portion of the sidewalk, muttering.

"But that's a pretty bad scare," Windrow said. "If she's that talented and that on the way up and that successful, his earnings off her contract could save years of subservience to Lobe. Even if he completely mismanages it, he should be able to sell it to somebody for a considerable amount of money."

Opium Jade considered this. "My man had to leave town once," she said after a pause. "He sublet my action to a friend of his for a percentage."

"Yeah," said Windrow bitterly. "Something like that. There are precautions against stuff like that, a clause to make any changes contingent on the artist's approval and so forth. But I've seen the contract Jodie signed with Lobe." He held up his thumb and forefinger. "It's about this thick. He could do anything he wanted, and it would probably stick."

They passed a beat cop who stood in a doorway pressing his radio's earplug tightly into his ear, listening intently. He recognized Windrow and raised his chin at him. When he saw Opium Jade he wagged his eyebrows, but continued to listen to his earplug.

"The thing is," Windrow continued, "it's a performance

contract. Lobe gets a cut of her performance work, and anything that grows out of it—a broadcast made of a performance, for instance. But he sees nothing from anything else. As far as I know, he receives no proceeds from her record—if there are any. If she doesn't perform, he doesn't earn anything off her."

"So what? That's to her advantage, isn't it?"

"Yes, it is good for her. But it would put the heat on Lobe to cash in on her before their contract expires. He probably thinks it's his natural-born right and duty to cash in on her. That's what employees are for, right?" He raised an eyebrow at Opium Jade.

"Lord, tell it," she sighed. "It's enough to make a body vote CWP."

"I thought you carried a card," Windrow said.

Opium Jade shook her head. "Just the one for the clinic, honey. One day Marx couldn't get it up anymore. A girl just don't know what to believe." She stopped and eyed a dress in a store window. Windrow stood beside her. Muzac drifted out of a speaker hidden above their heads. Opium Jade watched the dress quietly for a while, then focused on his eyes in the reflection in the window.

"I repeat. What makes you think somebody like her would have any need of a bum like you?" she said. "You don't think there's somebody hanging around the top of the heap can give her what she likes, how she likes, and shave every day in the bargain?"

Windrow looked through his reflection at the plastic legs of the coy mannikin. The feet had high heel shoes on them. A thin gold chain with tiny links twinkled on one ankle.

You're a cool drink in August, he said to himself, remembering Jodie Ryan's voice as she said it, her eyes two

inches from his. But he didn't speak. His eyes snapped into
focus with the image of Opium Jade's eyes in the window.
She looked at them for a minute.

"Oh boy," she said. "The dumb eyes of the helpless victim. You look like a deer caught in the highbeams on 101."
She put her arm through his and pulled. "Come on, I'll buy
you a glass of betadyne."

They entered the first licensed premises they came to. It
was a big one. The bar went from Market Street entrance
all the way to the back door, which opened onto Stevenson,
the alley fifty yards south. It was an old place, with a backbar
proscenium of carved mahogany pillars supporting a digni-
fied architrave that framed three shelves of bottles nearly as
long as the bar. It all looked and smelled just like 2 A.M. in
1923, in the little bit of smoky, ochre light allowed to penetrate. They had principles, too, to go along with the atmosphere. A beer with a shot went for eighty cents. Opium
Jade bought two each. She laid a two-dollar bill on the counter and told the huge red-faced Irishman on the other side,
complete with starched collar, pinstriped shirt, vest, sleeve
garters and a wrap-around apron hysted to his armpits, to
keep the change. He rapped his knuckles twice on the bar
and went away with the bill.

Opium Jade clicked her shot against Windrow's.

"Here's to love, goddamnit."

They drank.

A while later she went away and funded the jukebox and
came back. The antique Wurlitzer dated to Babbage. A lot
of electromechanical ruminations transpired before it got
down to playing a tune. The music itself filtered through
scratches and static after a loud thump and four introduc-
tory notes presaged the melody's imminent arrival.

John's in love with Joan
Joan's in love with Jim

Windrow looked sideways at Opium Jade. She sipped her shot and stared straight ahead.

Jim's in love with someone
Who's not in love with him

Windrow cleared his throat and tried to suppress a smile. The bass thummed and buzzed in the old box, lugubriously, yet with undeniable finesse.

What was meant to be must beeee
C'est la vie, c'est la vieeeee

Windrow's smile had turned into a grin. He put his hand on Opium Jade's shoulder and was about to speak when she shrugged it off.

Life's a funny thing
When it comes to love

Windrow frowned. He put his hand up to her chin and gently turned her face towards his.

You don't always conquer
The one you're thinking of

He was startled to see a tear fill the corner of her eye and glisten down her left cheek.

As they say
In old Paree

She moved her chin away from his fingers and stared over her shot at her own reflection, just visible in the mirror between the top and bottom of two rows of bottles.

C'est la vie
C'est la vie

"Fuck you, shamus," she said softly.

He looked away from her face to her reflection. Her eyes shone there, in the gloom among the bottles.

C'est laaa vieeee...

Chapter Thirteen

As Windrow negotiated the staircase that led to his office, gibbering voices held a conference in the shadows within and around him.

He couldn't make a lot of sense out of the chatter. He heard Opium Jade rendering bits of Verlaine, though she was now across the street, working, and he understood no French. He could hear Bdeniowitz berating somebody for a lousy job, no—wait—it was Bdeniowitz berating Windrow for doing a lousy job of being alive, snatches of a lecture delivered and received in the early seventies, when Windrow had still been a cop. He chuckled. He could still taste the humiliation of that night. The strains of a tune passed through his mind. He hummed to himself inaccurately. C'est la vie, c'est la vie. Aha. That laugh. Sal had laughed like that as she had removed her fist full of quarters from his stomach, in preparation for the blow that had rendered him unconscious. Had some quirk of her conscience chided her for decking this total stranger, and she'd laughed it off? Just as Windrow had guiltily laughed off Bdeniowitz' derision, years before?

Naw, he thought to himself. The laugh had been a by-product, a genuine expression let slip by mistake in the moment of enjoyment. Like a cry of love. Sure, that's it. Then had come the blow of redoubled ferocity that sent him over the desk. The laugh was extra, a filagree, an emotional tip.

He leaned on the bannister and breathed deeply. Nine dollars, sixty cents, plus tip. That's twelve of them. Six for Opium Jade, six for Windrow. Plus the round she bought. That made seven. Whew. He frowned. Beer and a shot, eighty cents? Crime. That's real crime, like taking brain cells from babies… He tried to remember whether or not he'd dipped into the two hundred dollars given him by Woodruff. Probably. Likely. Nine dollars, sixty cents. That's a lot of money. Plus tip. Have to fondle the resources, weigh carefully… Get that cash in the bank, cover that check to Bruce….

His head drifted with the smoky fumes of cheap Irish whiskey and draft beer.

He'd intended to extort information rather than money from Woodruff. But the fabrication about another will, that had meant something to the man.

"Here's a little something on retainer," he'd said, and winked. "You'll let me know the moment you find anything, of course." He'd damn near patted Windrow on the back. Golden retriever.

Windrow pulled one of the crisp hundred dollar bills out of his watch pocket. He couldn't read it but he stared at where its dim shape crackled between his fingers in the dark.

Not a lot of money. Just enough, maybe, to insure the loyalty of a shifty detective. That is to say, if you do find such a will, Mr. Windrow, be sure to let us be the first to see it. OK?

Windrow turned and sat on the edge of the second floor landing and stared down the dark stairwell, softly popping the C-note between his two hands like a shoeshine rag.

It seemed likely that somebody, somewhere would have

to know about any last will and testament for the document to be of any good to anyone. If old man O'Ryan had composed such a statement, there must be a lawyer holding it somewhere, or it must be someplace where it would be found. Anybody with a stake in it would apprise himself of its contents, which, if not already a matter of public record, would certainly come to light immediately upon the decease of the testator.

Maybe Woodruff had simply swallowed Windrow's story; could it be that simple?

Windrow made the hundred dollar bill snap, once, twice, and then it snapped neatly, accidentally, in two.

He reconstructed in the darkness beneath him the living room of Pamela Neil's house. He remembered the panelling, the maid, the piano, the red gemstone, the deafmute—and the paintings, each a portrait or an abstraction, with the single exception of the yacht over the mantle, and the oil well, on its way out. He saw the polished table covered with bottles of liquor, the sofas, the high windows in the western wall, the intricate rugs, the light on them.

He could see Pamela Neil, pretty but tired and thin, nervous and childish. Her button nose wrinkled when she sniffled. She sat with her knees drawn up and her legs to one side, held her drink beside her face in a hand whose elbow rested on her hip, the fingers straight up on the glass. She had told him nothing.

Nothing.

Here was a woman who had managed to marry herself an oil tycoon somewhere between two and three times her age, then divorce him. She liked cocaine, brandy, sailboats, had an aesthete for a boyfriend, a big house to keep him in, servants to wait on them. All she had to do was stay unmarried, so the alimony might keep rolling in.

Then the benefactor dies, she remarries, immediately her stepdaughter disappears, and a blackmailing detective shows up. What does she want? An explanation? An investigation? Paperwork? Security? A payoff?

No. She wanted a little fun.

So she hated herself. That was up to her. But why fool around with Windrow? Could she have been trying to spark Woodruff? No, probably not. She more than had her match in him. She'd stopped the unilateral eroticism when Woodruff returned from his telephone call with Jodie....

Now the phone call; that had been an interesting item. The smart tote would lay at least even money on the lies about that telephone call. Had it been Jodie? If so, did she say what Woodruff said she said? Windrow had been attacked minutes after he left their house. That meant two things: a) either he'd been followed there by the stolen limousine or, b) he'd been set up while he was there, in the house.

In either case, the telephone call could have been the tipoff.

That might mean that Woodruff had arranged to have himself called out of the room, which would mean the maid was in on it.

So. A talk with Concepción, the maid, might throw a little light on Woodruff's operation. She could say only one of two things: yes or no. If she says there was no phone call, the boss told me to interrupt you guys after you'd all settled in the living room? That would mean that Mrs. Neil had informed Woodruff of her telephone conversation with Windrow that morning, during which Windrow made the upsetting though vague suggestion about the future of their financial situation.

Mr. and Mrs. Woodruff. They'd gone and married after

the death of old man O'Ryan on the basis of the legitimate will. With the old man dead, the alimony or inheritance or whatever solidified, fixed forever, nothing stood between them and greenly padded marital bliss.

Or, if we have no incoming calls, what the hell was Woodruff doing out in the vestibule? If there were the slightest chance there might be a will superseding the probated one, the one that precipitated the marriage in Vegas, it would definitely be to Woodruff's advantage to get hold of it before anyone else. If that were so, why try to bump off Martin Windrow, the only person in the entire world claiming to know anything about it? Some way, some how, the will would turn up, if it existed. Bumping people off wouldn't solve anything, it was stupid, it only called attention to the anomaly. Whereas, hiring Windrow to ferret the document, that made sense. They would be stupid to suppress it, but if they got to it before anyone else, they could lay some plans accordingly. On the assumption that this Windrow is a cheap detective with only one thing in mind, the long green, you hire him to bird dog the document and bring it to his employer. Employer, naturally, will read the thing, out of curiosity, then forward it to the proper authorities. Of course. Genuine or not. Hard to believe the guy would go for it.

None of it added up to murder.

A long, low frequency blast from a ship's foghorn slowly filled the stairwell. Windrow suddenly noticed the chill in the air. A rat scratched at the baseboard along the hall corridor above, and something smelled dead. They never cleaned this place. Windrow moved his shoe against a stair tread. The scratching stopped. He folded his arms so that each hand was tucked into an armpit, a half of the C-note curled around each thumb.

How about a yes, phone call? Yes, Señor Windrow, there was a telephone call, and it was for Señor 'jefe' Woodruff, and pues, I think it might have been the Señorita Ryan. How many assumptions was that?

OK, he counted on his fingers. Woodruff was called to the telephone, because, yes, there was a call for him. Woodruff said it was the Ryan girl...

Windrow raised an eyebrow, and a corner of his mouth turned up ever so slightly. Someone who knew him well, observing carefully, might have said that he was smiling. But what he was thinking was the he'd referred to Jodie Ryan as the Ryan girl. Gone was the set of widening concentric circles on an otherwise undisturbed surface in a balmy climate, complete with kingfisher, a blue heron, a few egrets, crocodiles, jumping fish and spanish moss— commonly conjured at the mention of the word Jodie. He was still a sap for her, to be sure, and he'd be a sap the next time he saw her, if it were out of the context of this case. So his mind, finally, had discarded its preoccupation with its own wildlife—feathered and otherwise—wandering scientific in the fumes of nameless ethanol from County Cork. Ninety-sixty, plus tip. Eight rounds apiece. A cheap slap in the face.

The rat began scratching at the baseboard again.

If it had been the Ryan girl, that meant she would be the fourth person to be aware of Windrow's presence at the Neil house. And if she knew, Sal knew.

There was a resistance in him, somewhere, to that one connection, some kind of struggle. A duck disappeared off the quiet pond, pulled through the surface by a nimble tentacle. But he stared down the cold, dark stairwell, and listened to the rat gnawing above him. Right? he said to himself. Right mind? Think about it. If the Ryan girl knew Windrow was at the Neil house then Sal knew, and everybody, whoever they were, would say, *let Sal drive the car*, and Sal would let the steel creep molten into her eyes, and freeze there, her brain and cool hands drawing off the temperature, she would smile, and steal the car and run over Windrow with it. Wearing a white wig?

Could Jodie be on the wrong side in this?

Boojum, she'd called her granddad; a gentle, childhood sobriquet. Yet, undoubtedly, he was the man who'd discovered Sal, nurtured her. A man of affairs, such as Sweet Jesus O'Ryan, who liked to sit quietly in the desert, in a shack with no electricity, no running water, and read philosophy, while his empire flourished.

The whiskey he'd drunk earlier was wearing off. The tiny, dermal itch, which, when free, ran along the surface of his skin like a thin film of oxidation on a metal plate, lately erased by the alcohol, began again to tickle here and there, experimentally, at the corners of his temple and cheek. His thumbs crinkled the pieces of paper money. The rat's toenails clicked on the floorboards of the hallway.

He couldn't figure it. If she wanted him off the case, why had she called for help? Why the postcard? Until just a few minutes ago, all Jodie Ryan had to do was tell Windrow to stay out of her private life, and Windrow would happily have done so.

He tried to remember what case he'd been on the week before.

Ah, yes.

The swimming pool case.

A swimming pool had ruptured in Mill Valley.

Had the contractor who built it deliberately begun construction on uncompacted fill?

Lawyer Emmy Cohen had been retained by the home-owner.

She had put in a call to Windrow. It was still on his answering device.

He hadn't returned the call.

The rent was due.

He pulled his hands out of his armpits and looked at them in the dark.

One half to the landlord. It would be just what he needed to make up the difference between what he had in the bank and what he needed to make the rent. That left him a hundred and fifty dollars, mad money. A retainer. Forget Bruce.

The first thing to do would be to talk to Concepción. Bdeniowitz and Gleason had already done that, but they hadn't known about the telephone call, or its significance. Besides, they were stupid.

Another thing to do, contact Emmy Cohen, wish her good luck with the swimming pool, and get her to find a copy of Sweet Jesus O'Ryan's real will.

A third thing to do, maybe, was see if that red Ford would get him to Reward, California, and see what there was to see in O'Ryan's shack. Maybe talk to this Hardpan character about the old days.

Windrow frowned. A trip to the south end of the San Joaquin and back, with a little professional snooping at the far end, meant at least a day out of the city. He'd already lost a week to lethargy and the hospital. Would another day make any difference?

The freighter on the Bay emitted another long, low groan from its foghorn, a good thirty seconds worth. Its reverberations wafted investigatorily among the hard surfaces of the bricked canyons and paved gulches in downtown San Francisco, three, four, five; strong, long echoes.

Above him, the rat dropped some small item down the stairwell; it bounced off the first floor landing and hit the street door.

Windrow bit his lip. The time spent riding around in the desert would have to make a difference. The mere possibility of a second will had been enough to shake up Woodruff and Neil, perhaps enough for them to start killing people, if not each other. There must have been some other angle, something Windrow hadn't noticed....

He nodded his head in the dark, and tapped his foot on the stair tread. He had a cerebral rhythm, could feel nodes of it. He had some kind of metabolic empathy with its amplitude or period. He tapped his foot to let it know he was listening, to help it reappear on time, like a timed silence in the middle of a song presaged a consensus downbeat, three, four, and... Woodruff and Neil had some other problem related to O'Ryan's will, and Windrow's innocent lie had inadvertently reinforced their suspicions. Of course their idea of a second will, the possibility of its existence, perhaps a clue to its location, would be more real to them than to Windrow: Windrow had merely extemporized its existence, just to get a foot in the door, to have a look around. But they didn't know that. They'd been startled to hear that a total stranger had any idea of it. Startled, and maybe a little bit scared; panicked, even. If this guy Windrow knew about it, there was only one person he might have heard it from: Jodie Ryan.

Windrow pursed his lips. His emotional attachment to Jodie had led him to want to help her, to take the initiative when he'd thought her in trouble, but his fondness for Jodie had distracted him from a new possibility, that his little white lie had put Jodie on the spot.

At least two people, Woodruff and Neil, would have

wanted to ask her a question: namely, what's this about another will, *honey*?

Pamela Neil was dead. That left Woodruff.

Windrow stood up. It looked like the trip to O'Ryan's shack was inevitable. But what about that damned phone call?

He'd have to talk to Concepción before he left.

He fingered the two halves of the hundred dollar bill, turned, and strode down the hall to his office.

And pay the rent, he muttered to himself, searching in his pockets for his keys. Need some paper clips and a bottle of scotch, too. He put the two halves of the torn bill in one hand and rummaged in his pockets. No keys. He switched the paper into the other hand and found the keys in his left hip pocket, right where Opium Jade had playfully put them, after she'd snatched them from the ignition of the Ford, and while she'd kissed him goodnight.

He smiled, grimly, as he turned the key in the lock of his office door, and turned the knob.

Then he hit his head on the pebbled glass. The door hadn't opened. But, assuming it would after he'd unlocked it, he had walked right into it.

He ducked, flattened himself against the wall next to the door, and listened, scarcely breathing. He could hear nothing. Not even the rat made a sound.

Then the ship's horn again, a long, low, single note, a pause, then a short blast, that echoed up and down the street outside. Poking around in the fog, looking for a way out, an inarticulate urge in a befuddled mind.

Windrow looked at the keys dangling from the lock, still swinging slightly. Thinking his office door locked, he'd turned the key in the cylinder a full circle. That should have *unlocked* it. But it hadn't. Instead, he'd locked the door, which meant that someone had unlocked it and left it that way.

He waited, listening. He heard nothing. He smelled nothing. He saw nothing.

Down the hall, the rat began its nocturnal chores again. After a while, a truck chattered down Folsom Street.

After a long time, he admitted to himself what he already knew. If someone had been waiting to talk to him, they would have said something by now. If someone had wanted to shoot him, he'd already made himself a splendid target.

Logic is very reassuring.

Carefully, he reached up to the dangling keys and operated the lock. He turned the knob and pushed the door open.

Nothing happened.

He sprang out of his crouch and dove through the door. Something soft met him, something soft and... inanimate.

He put out his hands to help himself up, and one of them found a leg or an arm. He whimpered and recoiled. Soft and warm, with cloth around it. But not soft enough, and not quite warm enough.

He caused light with the switch and looked.

He was shaking. Better to be shot at than to embrace a dead body.

Concepción Alvarez would never tell him anything.

Chapter Fourteen

PETREL GLEASON STOOD OVER THE LIFELESS FORM OF Concepción Alvarez. He squinted down through the smoke of a cigarette whose drooping ash, though not extending quite so far, coped almost perfectly the curve his nose launched away from his face. He held his head to one side and maintained a recently wolfed hotdog in its place. His eyes were tired, multiple lines extended backwards from them toward each temple, discolored flesh encircled them, and the musculature that might pull his mouth into a smile didn't, but formed two deep downward clefts, one on each side of the descending corners of his mouth.

The smoke did not obscure his eyeful of death, no more than the sheet that covered her. The guts of flash bulbs fused to make a magnesium light that made the blue smoke bluer and the bright after-image of the sheet dance in his eyes. From a lower lip the camera spit out each stark image of an overlit, nameless room. A technician not as tired as Gleason, with a more clinical approach to sudden death, dusted white powder on the black telephone on Windrow's desk, revealing a solid mass of fingerprint whorls, and muttered Aha. Gleason shifted his eyes to the fingerprint man, held them there for a moment, then looked to the corpse.

He'd touched it earlier, when he'd first arrived, helping the coroner's assistant examine her. The neck was broken:

a job difficult to affect, but clean. She'd still been soft and warm, only her naturally dark color slowly leading the last changes, greying the rear guard of the body's sudden elision from life to death. He'd been reminded of a squirrel he'd found years before beneath a tree out of which it had fallen, still soft, still warm, the little machine winding down around the severed connection, its broken neck, its head dangling from the body like a sponge ball hanging by a rubber band off a wooden paddle.

Many cigarettes. Their butts lay crushed on the board floor around the front of Windrow's desk. The nicotine and the death brightened the effects of the light in the room. Light danced on the edges of everything except Windrow, who sat over a drink in a dark corner behind his desk, brooding silently.

In fact, Gleason wasn't sure if his perception of the light were attenuated by the horror of the scene, or the nicotine, or by the cocaine he'd filched from the ounce discovered at the scene of Pamela Neil's death. He hadn't been around long enough not to be surprised by this drug's particular superfluous qualities, but he had been around long enough to recognize in his nostrils the specific sting of methedrine. Mrs. Neil's cocaine had been heavily cut with speed. He'd not expected the powerful sting and the tears it brought to his eyes. He sniffled. Maybe it was dexedrine. You'd think a rich creampuff like her would have better connections. Anyway, being tired, he was grateful for the stimulus.

Windrow permitted a tic at one corner of his mouth to betray his amusement at the audible congestion in Gleason's nose, then forgot about it. The memory of colliding with the still warm body on the floor, where there should have been nothing but floor and maybe if only maybe a few bullets slapping overhead, eclipsed his indifferent opinion of

Gleason's mild indiscretions with the nose candy. Staying awake would always be a problem in Gleason's line of work, as it sometimes was in Windrow's, but thinking straight in the face of death presented a problem, too.

Windrow sat over his drink and stared at the corner of the sheet visible beyond the top of his desk. Periodically, one of the people from the crime laboratory passed between him and the body, muttering Latin undertones, but he took no notice of them. Twice he restrained himself from throwing his glass against the wall behind the door, a practice he'd found therapeutic in the past, when solutions or sense proved elusive, as now they seemed bent on proving themselves. He contented himself with imagining the amber rivulets of scotch following the wall down to the coving and the smashed bits of glass on the floor. There was some satisfaction to that.

Concepción Alvarez had been a pretty girl. Windrow knew that she was the sole surviving member of a large and politically active family from El Salvador, wiped out by way of a simpleminded solution to the differences between Right and Left. She'd been eighteen when it happened. Assured of a similar fate had she remained in her own country, she immigrated illegally to the United States with the idea of raising money to do the revolution some good.

After six months of poverty and culture shock, she'd gone to work for Pamela Neil at fifty dollars a week, plus room and board.

Jodie Ryan had a room in the basement of Pamela Neil's mansion. She used it when she was working in San Francisco. Concepción had a room just like it on the other side of the bathroom they shared. They became friends.

Jodie had described to Windrow how Concepción had covered the walls of her room with revolutionary posters, and surrounded her bed with books. For two years, while she worked for Woodruff and Neil, she educated herself. She taught herself English. Gradually, she had made herself aware of Che Guevara and Castro, of Benito Juárez and Zapata, of Thomas Jefferson, of Allende, Patrice Lamumba, Ho Chi Minh, the American, French, Chinese and Russian Revolutions, and other political and historical figures and processes. She discovered Sartre, Marcuse, Marx and the U.S. Constitution.

You know, Jodie Ryan had said to Windrow one day, it's not all theory with her.

Windrow had nibbled her ear and said, No? It isn't?

She told him that Concepción had found a man in Daly City who would sell anybody all the semi-automatic carbines anybody wanted for a hundred dollars apiece. Cash.

Windrow had shrugged. You got a buyer, you got a seller, you got a market. Interesting, but an old story. "Then she told me," Jodie had said, "that she knows Pamela Neil spends about four thousand a month on cocaine."

"One of the risks you run being extravagant," Windrow had pointed out, "is that there are always people out there somewhere who think they could spend your money a little more wisely than you do. Take the government, for example..."

"Right," Jodie had said. "I told her as much, and she walked out. I thought she'd left, and didn't really know what to do. Then she came back with a book and showed it to me. It was a collection of remarks by all kinds of people, philosophers mainly, opened to a particular page. The line she showed me said in effect, that the trick to being a servant is to rule the master."

"Was she referring to the situation in El Salvador, or did Concepción intend to become Pamela Neil's connection for cocaine?"

Jodie Ryan's shrugs were distracting. She shrugged a couple of times extra. "I don't know," she'd said after a while. "I offered an alternative, told her to skim a gram or two when the pile was big and it wouldn't be missed, and trade it for armaments. I even suggested we could stash the carbines in the attic until we could figure out how to ship them to El Salvador." She shrugged again. "I was feeling seditious."

"Well?"

"She said she wasn't too sure about becoming a gunrunner and a coke dealer all in one day; she'd have to think it over. That was the last I heard about it...."

Windrow hooked a drawer open with his foot and propped the other foot on it. His body creaked like an old oven door. On his desk in front of him lay the paperwork for two divorce cases and a breach of internal security in a burglar alarm company, and the two halves of the C-note. The edges of the former were beginning to curl and sunlight had yellowed the top sheets.

"Hey Gleason," he said, looking over the rim of his glass. "What's the quality of the Neil woman's stuff?"

Gleason coughed on his cigarette smoke, emitting a cloud between them. "How the hell would I know," he blustered.

Windrow put his glass on his desk and picked up a pencil. He tapped a rhythm on the glass with its tip. Gleason scratched his stubble.

Windrow raised his eyebrows and looked past Gleason at the door. "El Bad Ass'll be here any minute, Steve," he said. He shifted his eyes to his pencil, as he rolled it between his fingertips. Windrow was the only man Gleason knew who called him Steve. Even Gleason's wife had called him Petrel, right up until the day she left him.

Gleason looked halfway over his shoulder, at the lab

boys, then back at Windrow. "Been cut heavily," Gleason said. "Some kind of speed, dex probably. Not sure." He waved his cigarette hand. "Lab report's kind of vague."

There was a lot of noise in the hallway. The two or three reporters gathered there shouted questions; the police technicians looked busy. The uniformed officer outside Windrow's office let Max Bdeniowitz in, and restrained a couple of other people. A camera appeared over the heads of the knot of people at the door, its flash went off, the door closed against the moil. Bdeniowitz looked exactly like a man who thought he'd gotten away with going home and turning in early, then found out he hadn't.

"Hi chief," Gleason said cheerfully.

Bdeniowitz ignored him and addressed a coroner's assistant. "What happened?" he growled.

The coroner's assistant was a neat, young scientist with thin hair and gold rimmed spectacles, and his name was Michael. He frowned and picked a corner of his trim moustache. "Hard to tell exactly..." he began.

Bdeniowitz scowled. "You want *me* to tell *you*?"

"...but it looks like atlanto-occipual subluxation, subsequent to hemorrhage and swelling within the spinal cord, resulting loss of primitive functions leading to death." Michael spoke primly and continued to curry his moustache, while looking at the corpse.

"Broken neck," Bdeniowitz muttered. "She fall?"

"Nope."

"Pushed?"

"Nope."

"Well?"

"Some kind of hold, executed by a strong, inexpert person. I'm guessing. They struggled."

"Man or woman?"

The coroner's assistant shook his head.

"Anything else?"

The man showed a tentative expression and waggled the fingers of one hand, palm down. "Could have been right-handed," he said.

"Great. A strong right-handed inexperienced person. Gleason."

Gleason consulted his small spiral-bound notebook. "Got the call 9:10, arrived 9:20. She was there, Windrow was there." He pointed at Windrow behind the desk. "Says he came in at 9:05 or so and found her where she lies. No weapons on the premises, except for Marty's .38," he pointed at the pistol on top of the file cabinet. "unfired. Says he wasn't carrying it. He pulled it out of a file drawer when I asked after it." He replaced the notebook in his pocket. "No signs of forced entry, no signs of a struggle. Windrow says the place wasn't searched."

Bdeniowitz looked at Windrow, his face sour. "Nothing missing?"

Windrow shook his head.

"Why you?"

Windrow shook his head.

Bdeniowitz' eyes flared and the knots at his jaw hinges puffed up. "Look, apple, I know you know who this is, at least."

Windrow nodded. Gleason spoke up.

"Say it's," he consulted his notebook, "Concepción Alvarez. Pamela Neil's maid."

Bdeniowitz inhaled slowly and exhaled a long, loud sigh. "Pamela Neil," he said, nodding to himself. "Apple..."

"Nice little farm in a warm climate with goats and a woman don't speak English?" Windrow suggested helpfully.

"If you don't give us any help on this apple, I'll see if I can arrange it. Was she dead when you got here?"

Windrow nodded.

"What she want?"

"She didn't say."

"She leave anything? A message, a phone number? Ever talk to her before?"

Windrow shook his head.

"C'mon, dammit. Why you?"

"I'm as in the dark as you are, Max. All I can figure is she must have known something about Pamela Neil's death and she figured to tell me about it. But there's another angle."

Bdeniowitz tried to look interested.

"She might have known something about Jodie Ryan's whereabouts."

"So?"

"She knew we were friends."

"So what about Jodie Ryan's whereabouts?"

"I'm working on it."

"What you got."

"Nothing. A sore back." Windrow poured himself two fingers of scotch. Bdeniowitz raised his eyebrows, then narrowed his eyes. "Scrape your knuckles getting that jug off the shelf?"

Windrow didn't look at the knuckles of his right hand. He'd split the skin over two of them on Harry Lobe's face. The abrasions reopened when he'd rolled through the office door. He stood the bottle in the open desk drawer.

"I had to tap a guy out earlier today," he said indifferently.

Gleason showed Bdeniowitz his notes. Bdeniowitz skimmed them and scowled.

"Big day for you, apple. You get out the hospital from being almost killed, pick up a hooker, go a couple rounds with somebody on the way to the bar, where you get toasted, drop off the hooker, then trip over a stiff in your front door.

Did I get it all?" He indicated the form under the sheet, without waiting for an answer. "Suppose you get a little more specific."

"It doesn't matter," Windrow said gloomily.

"Let me be the one gets depressed about it doesn't matter."

Windrow shrugged. "Guy named Lobe tried to shoot his way out of talking to me. I had to sit him down."

Before the words were out of his mouth, Windrow realized he'd spilled beans he hadn't even known he was holding, because Gleason and Bdeniowitz exchanged meaningful glances, a rare occurrence.

Bdeniowitz cocked his head and eyes to one side, licked his lips, then looked at Windrow again.

"You did what?" he said carefully.

"I, uh, had to hit him," Windrow held up the knuckles, then raised a forefinger. "Once."

Bdeniowitz examined a fingernail. "This guy Lobe, apple. That wouldn't be Harry "Greased" Lobe? Pimp, loan shark, snowman, 15 percenter? Billed himself a theatrical agent? Same guy you sat down, this afternoon?"

A small, pointed light bulb, the 1.5 volt kind you see a lot of around Christmas time in the windows of discrete antique stores, with the curly tip, unfrosted, lit up above Windrow's head. "Lobe is a cocaine dealer?"

Bdeniowitz put his hands on his hips, pushing back his coattails as he did so, revealing the snub-nose revolver clipped to his belt. "I asked you first, apple. Answer the question."

"Yeah," said Windrow impatiently, "Yeah. Same guy. Harry Lobe, Lobe Theatricals. Has a cell down on lower Turk, third floor in the back, over the love-toy dealer. He's a coke dealer?"

"What an act," Gleason grumbled.

"About what time of day were you employing your sit-down technique on the Greased Lobe, apple?"

Windrow thought about it. "Maybe three o'clock this afternoon?" He looked at his wristwatch. "Matter of fact, it was three oh five." He tapped the crystal with a fingernail. "My watch must have stopped when I hit him."

Bdeniowitz waited. Gleason licked his fingertips and went through the pages of his notebook.

"Well?" Bdeniowitz said impatiently.

Gleason stopped on a page and ran a finger down the lines. "Two fifty-five," he read. He looked at Windrow. "Your watch was fast, you hope."

"Could be, but..."

"Or he's lying," Bdeniowitz observed.

"Maybe it didn't stop right away. Maybe——." Windrow looked back and forth at the two of them. After what must have seemed a long time to them—it did to him—, he made the connection.

"So Lobe's dead too," Windrow said.

The two detectives stared at him.

Chapter Fifteen

"SOMEBODY PUT A BOMB IN THE MAN'S WASTEBASKET," Bdeniowitz explained. "Consisted of a bundle of dynamite, a windup alarm clock with nails stuck in the face, a lantern battery and a detonator. Maybe some other stuff. It's hard to tell. We found the battery nearly intact on the roof of the building behind Lobe's, but not much else." He sighed. "In fact, it was a hell of a job figuring out whether or not the victim was actually Lobe. But the lab boys, they found Lobe's dentist and enough teeth to do the match."

Michael, the coroner's assistant, leaning against the wall near the door, pushed his spectacles onto his forehead and scrubbed his eyes with his hands.

"We kicked it over," Windrow said thoughtfully.

"Kicked what over?"

"The wastebasket. In the fight. We kicked it over, some trash spilled out, crumpled up bills and papers, brown paper bags, and a 1/2-gallon milk carton..." Windrow quickly sketched his encounter with Lobe that afternoon, describing how he and Sister Opium Jade had tricked Lobe into letting them into his office, how Lobe pulled a gun on them, how they wrecked the office in the ensuing struggle. "When it was over, one of the first things he did was stand up the wastebasket. Half the stuff in it was on the floor."

Bdeniowitz shook his head in disgust. "Leave it to the apple to have a whore as his alibi."

"Hey," said Windrow, "she's a nice girl."

"What is it with you and the chippies, apple? Every time you..."

"Look, I told you what she was doing there, and I told you what I was doing there. You don't believe me, go ask the girl. You don't believe her, you can ask me again. Anybody with brains to think with can see we damn near got blown up with Lobe."

Gleason sucked on a cigarette. "You think somebody was out to get the two of you?"

Windrow shook his head. "Nobody knew I was heading for him. I left headquarters and drove straight here, collected the girl. We cooked up the story on the way to Turk Street, parked, went calling on Lobe."

"They were after Lobe," said Bdeniowitz. But he was frowning. "There's only one hole in your story, apple."

"The one in my shoe?" Windrow tried to look hopeful.

Bdeniowitz shook his head. "The last page of Lobe's appointment calendar, apple. One of those jobs with the big rings, has two pages for every day of the year and time slots?" He waved at Gleason. "We found it in the office upstairs, next to the hole in the floor."

Gleason had his notebook ready. "Only notation for today," he said, "was for capital M period capital W period," he lowered the notebook and looked at Windrow, "at 2:00 this afternoon."

Windrow looked from Gleason to Bdeniowitz and back and held up his hands: "So he had a masseuse called the Merry Widow."

Gleason stifled a laugh.

"Yeah," said Bdeniowitz sourly. "The Merry Widow."

Windrow shook his head. "If the guy was clairvoyant he was a half hour off," he said. "The girl didn't even know where we were going until we got there, and I didn't feel any intelligent vibrations probing my subconscious on the way over.

"What about the initials?"

"How should *I* know?" Windrow shouted. "I got my rocks off hitting the guy in the face. You guys know damn well I don't sport bombs in wastebaskets. Get off it. Go through his records and see what M.W.'s he had a piece of. From what I hear they would have plenty of reason to want to blow him up...."

The coroner's assistant interrupted, wanting to know if he could move the corpse.

"Keep your goddam shirt on," Bdeniowitz snapped. "Johnson!" he shouted. The uniformed officer standing guard outside Windrow's door came in, holding the door shut behind him.

"Go across the street and bring them three hoses over here."

Johnson looked at Bdeniowitz and did nothing.

"What the fuck you looking at?" Bdeniowitz shouted. "Go get those three chicks standing in the door across the goddam street and bring em here! Now!" His face turned purple.

"Y-yessir," the officer said, and left.

"Watch the door, Gleason," Bdeniowitz turned on Windrow. "If this fluff don't corroborate every syllable of your line, I'm taking every goddam one of us downtown and we're gonna stay there til we get it straight. I'm sick if this shit. You been a walkin' Peckinpah script for a week and if something don't break in this case, there won't be nobody but you and me left to hang for it."

Windrow opened his mouth.

"Shutup," Bdeniowitz snarled.

Bdeniowitz extracted one half of a large cigar from his inside coat pocket and Gleason torched it for him. Silence and smoke filled the room while Bdeniowitz smoked and paced. Windrow got up and added some ice to his scotch. Both he and Bdeniowitz had to step around the body lying in the middle of the room. Gleason leaned against the door and glumly chewed a cigarette.

After a while, they heard appreciative voices in the hallway and a loud wolf whistle. The door moved behind Gleason, and he stepped aside to let in Sister Opium Jade, Marlene and Candy, the three prostitutes who worked the entrance to the grocery store across Folsom Street. Michael, the coroner's assistant straightened his glasses and cleared his throat. At Bdeniowitz' direction Gleason closed the door on Johnson and the reporters beyond, who fired a lot of bulbs and yelled a lot of inquiries.

The three women came in with their faces set to weather whatever the police had in mind, but none of them was prepared to look at a corpse. They all gasped and became noticeably upset. Sister Opium Jade looked helplessly from the sheeted form on the floor to Windrow, her eyes begging him to get her out of there. Windrow, seated behind his desk again, said nothing.

"Well, ladies," Bdeniowitz began, sitting on his heels and raising a corner of the sheet. "Any of you seen this woman before?"

Candy hid her face, sobbed, and refused to look. Sister Opium Jade stared in silent horror. Marlene nodded slowly, her mouth open, then shook her head.

"That means yes or no?" Bdeniowitz asked her.

"N-no," the woman stuttered. "I mean, she could have

been the one came in the building tonight, couple hours ago."
She tore her eyes from the corpse and looked at Windrow.

"Tell the man what he wants to know."

"That's all there is. A couple of hours ago. She was the
only person I noticed since five o'clock, coming in. Everybody else was coming out, and there wasn't anybody at all
since about six. Other than that, it was just the usual cow-
boys and leather freaks up and down this goddam street."

Windrow frowned.

"Got dark around six, didn't it?" he observed.

"Yeah," Marlene agreed bleakly. "Getting late in the year."
She shivered visibly and wrapped her thigh-high squirrel coat
tighter around her. As she half turned away from the corpse
on the floor, she looked old and tired. In her coat, big earrings,
makeup, mini-skirt, nylon encased legs and stacked heels, she
also looked ridiculous.

Bdeniowitz dropped the corner of the sheet and stood
up. "Anybody else?"

Sister Opium Jade, who had also turned away from the
grisly sight, shook her head. "I got here about half an hour
before you guys showed up." She jerked her head toward
Windrow, started to say something, changed her mind.

Bdeniowitz caught it. He looked from Opium Jade to
Windrow and back again. "Yeah?" he snarled.

"Tell him." Windrow said, "where you were."

"I was with him." She shrugged, "and I was too drunk to
sep across the street."

Gleason clucked his tongue.

"Where?" said Bdeniowitz. "When? How?"

She told him the rest of the story, leaving out most of
the violence.

When she finished, Candy whirled on her and said, "You
told me he pounded Lobe into the floor and left him for dead!"

Sister Opium Jade looked daggers at her and said nothing.

"Dead, eh?" Bdeniowitz said.

Windrow smiled at Opium Jade behind Bdeniowitz' back.

"I told you that cause I knew you wanted to hear it," Opium Jade said, not too comfortably. She looked at Bdeniowitz. Bdeniowitz looked at her. "Candy used to work for Lobe," she explained. "Secretary."

"Hah!" Gleason said.

"He was a louse and she hates the guy. Marty only had to hit Lobe once after he threw him through the door..." she stopped and bit her lip. Bdeniowitz looked at Windrow, who wiped the grin off his face, and back to Opium Jade. "Go on," he said. "Fill in the blanks."

"Well, I knew that just wouldn't be enough for Candy in the straight telling of it. You just had to've been there." She cranked her hand around her wrist a couple of times. "It was OK live, but I just kind of jazzed the replay up for her, make her feel good."

"Shit," said Candy.

"Well," Opium Jade shrugged. "You get bored standing on the lousy corner, and it's cold, too. All those creeps driving by looking to do weird things to you, a girl wants a little conversation to keep her nerve up..."

"You told me he creamed that jerk like hot black coffee!" Candy screamed. "You told me—"

"Sometimes it's like talking to yourself out there, goddamn company's so goddamn stupid..."

"—Lobe'd never walk or talk or fuck again your lousy dick friend crippled that scum for—"

"...discussing wigs and genitalia for godsakes..."

They went on like that for a while, being good at it. Bdeniowitz, however, had seen it more times than they'd performed it and patiently ignored them. Everybody in the room knew the two women were arguing just to avoid discussing anything factual. Finally he jerked the office door open and pushed Candy and Marlene past Johnson into the hallway. Flashbulbs popped and questions filled the air.

"Hey," said Marlene, backing out of the door behind Candy, "doncha wanta take a statement or nothing?"

"We'll be in touch," said Bdeniowitz, pushing her into the hall. "Johnson."

"But what about my important material evidence?" she said, smoothing her dress over her hip.

Bdeniowitz ignored her. "Johnson. Escort these ladies to their side of the street."

"Not you," Bdeniowitz said, stepping between the door and Sister Opium Jade. "You stick with us for a while longer."

A reporter had backed Candy up against the far wall of the hallway, leaning his elbow on the wall, and was explaining his research for a big feature on prostitution, in low not to say furtive tones, as Bdeniowitz closed the door.

Bdeniowitz quickly established that Sister Opium Jade had been with Windrow for most of the afternoon and evening, until he'd left her in front of the grocery across the street at about eight thirty. He tried a few angles, mostly veiled threats, but couldn't shake her. The coroner's assistant allowed as how he thought the deceased had been that way since at least eight, possibly earlier. Bdeniowitz finally ordered him to remove the body.

The two coroner's assistants produced a black rubber bag and zipped the body into it. Then they strapped it onto a stretcher, and departed with it through the crowd stacked up against the office door. Flashbulbs popped in the hall. Nobody said much until after the door had closed again.

Then Gleason said, "Hey." He walked over to the front of Windrow's desk and picked up a light blue three by five card that lay within the chalked perimeter marking where the body had been. He handled the card by its edges.

"This yours?" he said, and showed the card over the desk to Windrow.

One side of the blue card was blank, the other had two lines Windrow recognized as Greek, though he had no idea of what they said, carefully hand-lettered in white.

$$\text{Τοῦ γαρ δούλουη Τέχνη αρχει Τοῦ δεδηοΤοῦ}$$
$$-\text{Διογενε}$$

Gleason stepped, behind the desk to look at the card over Windrow's shoulder. "It must have been under the girl's body."

Windrow studied the card for a few seconds, then shook his head. He looked at Sister Opium Jade who, with Bdeniowitz, was looking at him. He took the card from Gleason, holding its edges between his finger tips, and showed it to Sister Opium Jade. "Greek," she said. *Tou gar douloua technae archei tou desnotou. —Diogenes*.

Everybody except Windrow came on surprised.

Gleason swiveled his head from Sister Opium Jade to Windrow and back again. "Easy for you to say, Sister," he muttered.

"What's it mean, goddamit," said Bdeniowitz, exasperated.

"'The art of being a slave is to rule one's master.'" She handed the card to Gleason. "Diogenes was the name of the guy who said it."

Everybody stared at the educated streetwalker.

Windrow stared at her too, but he was also recalling a bit of pillow talk with Jodie Ryan.

"You know," Opium Jade coaxed, "the guy with the lantern?" She held one hand over her head and looked from one blank face to another.

"Skip it," she muttered, lowering her hand.

"The art of being a slave is to rule the master," Gleason repeated, as if to himself. "What the hell does that mean?"

"Right now, this Alvarez girl is looking pretty artless," Bdeniowitz adduced bitterly, staring at the outline chalked on the bare floorboards in front of Windrow's desk. "No matter what it means."

Chapter Sixteen

THE SPEEDOMETER ON THE RED FORD SHIMMIED AROUND 110. The motor seemed to like it, and Highway 5 unreeled like a hallucinated ribbon behind him. The front end floated a bit at that speed, like a small boat working its way against a mild swell, but the steering still worked when he passed the slower traffic. And all the traffic was slower, with one exception. This was a black Ferrari that passed him just south of the Los Banos turnoff. Doing perhaps twenty or thirty miles an hour better than his car, it used the visible fifteen miles bisected by Windrow's mirror and windshield in a little over six minutes, threading its nocturnal trace among the San Francisco-to-L.A. freight and produce trucks as if it were a sleek, gravityless wedge mysteriously propelled by its own lights through so much cubist furniture. Some of the trucks, illuminated in red, green and amber, like carnival booths, twinkled their lights appreciatively at the Ferrari and even Windrow's Ford, as they flashed in turn down the fast lane. Shortly after the Ferrari passed him a Highway Patrol car also passed him, all its lights going, a thin plume of smoke spiralling out of one of its two exhaust pipes. At that moment, going slightly uphill, Windrow's speedometer read over 100.

Though he accelerated to 110, the CHP cruiser left him behind.

After everybody had departed his office, a few telephone calls provided Windrow with a few hard facts.

Though she was a little drunk when he finally found her at a Malibu number, Jodie Ryan's mother, Kitty Larkin, happily answered everything Windrow cared to ask her. Yes, though she wasn't aware of the specific terms of O'Ryan's will, she knew he'd left her out of it entirely. But, she'd cheerfully pointed out, that was OK by her. She and her father hadn't spoken since she had married her third husband, because her third husband was in the movie business, Jewish, and rich. Toward the first two categories O'Ryan had begun to manifest an unreasonable animosity in his later years, and that her present husband's money made Kitty Larkin—who had grown to expect a 'minimum standard of excess,' as she put it, assuring Windrow he understood these things— independent of O'Ryan's influence, had further irked Sweet Jesus to the point that he wrote her out of his will.

Kitty Larkin, she explained to Windrow, the ice in her glass tinkling near the mouthpiece of the telephone, had not resented her father's behavior toward her, which she described as 'peevish,' but merely reduced her direct communications with him to annual Christmas and birthday cards since 'at least ten years ago.'

Their excision from the will, Windrow thought at the time, might explain why Kitty Larkin and her husband had experienced no unusual activities in their lives since O'Ryan's death. They had received no threatening telephone calls, there had been no burglary, no violence... "Just the usual small arms fire," Mrs. Larkin had observed, "down on the beach at night." The ice clicked again. "Marijuana smugglers you know, landing bales in the quiet residential areas, only to encounter pirates waiting for them. Not a damn one of them over seventeen."

The smugglers or the pirates?

"Neither. Both. Whatever. Jodie... You know, Mr. Windrow, Jodie has told me quite a lot about you, and, although you're not really of our circle, socially I mean, I must say you seem an interesting man." She laughed, a full, deep laugh. "Please don't be offended, that wasn't what I meant to say at all... Heavens, I think I'm getting tipsy. No, what I meant to tell you was that Jodie named herself for the old man's first wife, you know. The one who left him when he went broke the first time, Jodie Dweem. She went back to Philadelphia. Broke his heart. He never forgot her. Named his damned oil wells after her, and tried to get his second wife, my mother, to name *me* after her. Of course, for all she cared, he could have named those marvelous oil wells after the saints and the Holy Family if he'd wanted to, but as for naming her own flesh and blood after that woman, well: momma absolutely wouldn't stand for it, poor thing. He sprung it on her when she was still in the hospital, with me in the incubator— I was born a tad early, it *must* explain my absolutely smashing figure, knock on wood."

He heard the tap of her glass against the tabletop.

"Of course she wouldn't stand for it. Can you imagine? Right in the damned hospital. She finally left him after they bought a mansion in Beverly Hills and he tried to call it Jodieland, or something. Absolutely the last straw. Of course," she added, with a chuckle, "she got the mansion in the settlement, lock, stock and barrel-chested chauffeur, and raised all of us lovely neurotic children there, and called it Tara. Does that answer your question?"

"Yes ma'am," said Windrow, scratching the stubble on his throat. "What I really need to know is how to get to the shack your father died in, and where I might find this fellow Hardpan. Also, do you have any idea where Jodie is?

And what do you know about a woman—I think she's a woman—called—."

"Sal? Oh, you must mean Sal."

"Sal, yes ma'am."

"Well, Mr. Windrow, I don't see Jodie much, and certainly not since Dad died. She stays here sometimes, when she's singing in L.A., but not too often. Last time would have been this past summer, I think. She was here for about two days."

"You don't get along?"

"Oh, we get along alright. But Jodie is determined to make her own career, her own money, her own way. Hal, my husband, Hal offered to help her when they first met, and she jumped all over him! Naturally I was rather sharp with her at the time, and she's been in a qualified snit ever since. I think I understand her, but really, the way she thumbs her nose at *millions*—well..." Mrs. Larkin sighed. "So, I don't see much of Jodie, as she calls herself. But she still calls regularly enough."

"So, Jodie was close to your father?"

"Very. I haven't seen his will, or Jodie to ask her, but I'll bet he left most of the shooting match to her." She sighed again. "I hope she has the sense to ask Hal for some advice, at least, I fear she'll find it very difficult to be a business tycoon *and* a nightclub singer."

"And Sal?"

"Oh yes. Sal. Would do anything Edward would tell her to. She was his bodyguard, if you can believe it."

Windrow touched the sore side of his face. "I can believe it."

"Among other things."

"What other things?"

"She used to keep an eye on Jodie, for one. Always

knew where she was, who she was shacking up with, how her career was doing. That sort of thing. Whenever Daddy would hole up in the desert place, Sal would keep tabs on Jodie until he got ready to go public again."

"What would he do there, while he was holed up?"

"Read. His first wife, the original Jodie, always made him feel inferior about his education. That and his financial status. I never met her and don't want to, if she's still alive, but from what I understand, she must have been quite a bitch. I mean, when I was a kid, before mother threw daddy over for the house and the chauffeur, he came into my room drunk one night and sat on the edge of the bed to say goodnight, and I asked him about this Jodie business—you know, how come we had a mare called Jodie, and the pump sites. Well, he cried. I'll never forget it. He sat there drunk as could be and just blabbered about this Jodie, how beautiful she was, how educated she was, what good family she came from—in the *strangest* tone of voice. I was five years old and it scared me sick. Later on I thought about it, and realized that, as of that night, he must not have seen or heard from the woman in over fifteen years. Yet, he cried like she'd died in his arms at the Battle of the Alamo or something."

A short silence ensued, during which Mrs. Larkin did not take a drink. Windrow said nothing.

"So anyway," she resumed, "he would always read a lot, not only technical books about oil drilling and grain futures and things, you know the kind of stuff, but also a lot of philosophy, history, the Latin poets and statesmen, Plutarch and Cicero and their ilk." she giggled. "Writers and thinkers of the first water, as my second husband used to say."

"Diogenes?" Windrow asked, fishing.

"Mm," she said. "He was Greek, wasn't he? I don't

know but I would say Daddy probably read Diogenes. And Socrates and Heraclitus and Homer and Suetonius and plenty of others. This woman Jodie actually shamed him into becoming an educated man, much more educated than I could imagine her being. His success too, was probably motivated by her rejection of him, at least in part. That man could work harder and longer than anybody I ever met and honey," she clucked her tongue twice, as if urging a horse through its paces, "I've met a few. Jodie inherited that penchant for work."

Windrow cleared his throat. "Anything else about Sal?"

"Totally loyal to Sweet Jesus O'Ryan. I don't know what she's doing now, or who's she's working for, but it's a cinch that daddy told her how it would be when he was gone. Now he's gone, that's the way it is, if she has any to do with it."

"Did you go to the funeral?"

"Can't stand 'em, honey. I send flowers. Roses. Red roses, if it's a woman. Yellow roses for the boys."

"Ahm—" Windrow began.

"Yellow cause I figure they just kept a date with somebody else, and I'm jealous."

"What color did O'Ryan get?"

"He was a man, yellow, same as the rest. Maybe a better man, actually. I always was a tad jealous of that first Jodie, when I was younger. Almost like she broke up our home personally. Yeah. . . . Yellow."

She gave him directions to O'Ryan's place, and the name of a cafe in Taft in which Hardpan had been seen between five and six o'clock every morning for thirty years.

"Thanks for all this time, Mrs. Larkin."

"Think nothing of it," she had said cheerily, "it's been fun getting sloshed and nostalgic over Daddy, bout time

I gave him a proper wake. I guess this'll be all the mourning the son of a bitch gets out of me."

Windrow thought he heard the hint of a catch to her voice. He'd nearly hung up when he'd thought to ask what she might know about Pamela Neil and Woodruff.

"She got red ones," she said, "even though I hadn't seen Pam and Manny since Jodie's first big performance in L.A. A dump called the Shotgun, about five years ago.... Disgusting place. Cement floor, stank of beer, too loud...."

About to pour himself another drink, Windrow almost let the name go by.

"Manny?" he said, the bottle poised over the glass.

"Woodruff," said the lady from Malibu. "Manny Woodruff. How do you think they met? Pamela and Woodruff, I mean. It was at a party at my house. Daddy was holed up in the desert, see, and Pamela got tired of sitting around the San Francisco place... Or was it the Carmel place? I can't remember. Anyhow, whenever she got bored, she'd hang around with Jodie or me or both of us. Unless she had something going on the side, of course. A fella, I mean. After all, Daddy was in his seventies and she wasn't thirty yet, to hear her tell it. She wasn't very particular about hiding the boys from me and Jodie, and, hell, I understood the—"

"What about Woodruff?" Windrow said, putting the bottle down.

"They met at a party at my house. Bango, just like that. And I do mean bango. That was right before he sold a faked Matisse to some big producer. About a year later the guy had it authenticated and, sure enough, it was a de Houry. *Beautiful* picture. Too bad he didn't hang onto it. Now it's worth almost as much as the real thing since deHouri killed hims—."

"So who called him Manny?"

"Why darling *everybody* in L.A. called him Manny. Of course he had to close the Laguna Beach Gallery after the stink that ignorant producer raised over the fake painting, but Manny rode that one out. He's no dummy, either. The customer dropped the charges when Manny bought the picture back. His reputation was ruined around here, but by then Pamela was all his. He moved to San Francisco to be with her and took it easy for a while. After de Houry got famous Manny got a little local press about his picture, sold it for a lot of money, and picked up a reputation for a sharp eye to boot. After Pammy divorced Sweet Jesus, Manny opened a new gallery with the proceeds—one would imagine a little help from Pamela's annuity—and started to clean up peddling unknown abstract expressionism like some people peddle vacuum cleaners—every house needs at least *one*, right?"

"Manny," Windrow murmured.

"Good old Manny, dearie. Is there anyone else in my immediate or not so immediate circle you'd like to gossip about? Hmmm?" she hiccupped. "Excuse me."

"No thank you ma'am, not just now. If I think of anything else I'll give you a call."

"Love to hear from you darling. So lovely to have met you. Ta."

They hung up.

He sat in his office, not moving, not drinking, just sitting, for about fifteen minutes. Then he stirred the coke and speed into his glass of whiskey. While the mixture spun in the glass, he made two more calls. One to Gleason, to give him the tip about Woodruff's nickname, which tied Woodruff, circumstantially at least, to the initials in Lobe's appointment book. Gleason promised to obtain a warrant to search Woodruff's gallery.

"Oh—Steve?"

"Yeah, Marity?"

Windrow lifted the glass. "Thanks for the bump."

"Anytime, baby."

The last phone call went to Emmy Cohen, the lawyer. Emmy Cohen and Windrow took turns employing each other. She promised to pull strings in order to discover the terms of Sweet Jesus O'Ryan's will. Windrow promised to call back, soon.

Then he drank the amphetamine, or methedrine, or dexadrine, or whatever it was the cocaine had been cut with, dissolved in whiskey.

The solution numbed his esophagus, loosened his bowels, and woke him up.

Now the Ford roared beneath him.

Chapter Seventeen

OUTSIDE THE FORD IN THE MOONLIT DARKNESS THE SAN
Joaquin Valley flowed north, taking with it mile after mile of
aqueducts, Los Banos, the Pacheco Pass, the potential site of
Los Vaqueros Reservoir, the San Luis Reservoir and Forebay,
sizzling power transit lines, 43% of California agriculture, the
intersection where James Dean died, the stench of herbivore
dung that envelopes a few cubic miles around the huge Harris
Ranch feedlot at the Coalinga turnoff, gas flares, blue mercury
lights and the sulphurous reek peculiar to the oil fields that
dot the whole valley with increasing density until the traveler
arrives in that unique oilrich pocket in the southern San Joaquin, between the westward-curving southern tip of the Sierra
Nevada and the slopes of the easternmost Coastal Ranges, in
western Kern County, California.

Here the traveler finds oil wells and walking beam pumps
everywhere; in backyards, next to restaurants, in supermarket
parking lots, in cotton fields and pastures and fruit groves, on
desert flats: multiply in fields or preserved as relics, like a val-
ued species of shade tree. In the first third of the twentieth
century, California produced more oil than any other state, and
a great deal of it came from the south end of the San Joaquin
Valley.

It was into the vertiginous financial prospects of oil, the
ruthlessness of water politics, and the dizzying manipula-

tion of irrigable land that Edward "Sweet Jesus" O'Ryan had inserted himself by his sentimental purchase of an insignificant plot of desert in the thirties. Deepwell technology turned his innocuous purchase into a small empire. As Windrow negotiated the Buttonwillow turnoff he was mulling over the luck of old man O'Ryan, and the shortsighted willfulness of his proud bride from Philadelphia.

But Windrow had been driving at speed for almost three hours, and found himself underestimating the curve of the off ramp. He passed the 35mph sign doing better than seventy, slid sideways up to and slightly beyond the stop sign at the end of it, before he got the machine halted. Across the road stood an open gas station, empty of traffic, with a young attendant sitting bolt upright in a chair next to a pump staring in unabashed, open-mouthed admiration at Windrow's smoking Ford. Windrow drove a crescent to the pump island, switched off the motor, and got out and stretched, wide awake.

The kid eagerly washed every window, inside and out, filled the empty tank with hi-octane solvent, and dumped two quarts of black gold into the creaking engine block. He'd checked every fluid reservoir on the car and had three tires properly inflated when Windrow returned from the telephone booth at the other end of the lot. The detective paced around the pump island, lost in thought, while the kid brought the fourth tire up to snuff, readjusted his Crane Racing Cams cap and reported in.

"You need some brake fluid, mister. Water's ok in the battery and radiator. She took two quarts of oil and seventeen and a half gallons of gas, the right rear—"

"Put it in," Windrow waved his hand at the car.

The kid pulled a can of brake fluid out from under the rag hanging out of the back pocket of his coveralls and topped off the reservoir, saying the while, "Also, sir, I couldn't help but notice your fan belt squealing as you pulled across the intersection, I can take care of that for you two ways sir, though you seem to be in a hur—"

"How long's the quick way?"

"About three seconds, sir, you just—"

"Do it."

The kid drooled some of the brake fluid out of the can onto his fingers and pinched them around the inside circumference of the tired fan belt, rubbing it in, observing as he did so, "You handle this rig pretty good, sir, if I may say so, though I imagine she oversteers like a motherfucker—"

Windrow handed thirty dollars to the kid. "That cover it?"

Windrow was traveling faster than the kid was, who was falling far enough behind that he took the cash with the same hand that had brake fluid all over it.

"Yessir," he said, disappointed that Windrow didn't want to discuss driving techniques. "I'll get your change."

"Keep it," Windrow said, slamming the hood. "Which way is Reward, California?"

The attendant pointed west. "Highway fifty-six to McKittrick, take the right into the hills."

"The right?"

"There's only one, sir."

"Thanks for the service," Windrow said, getting into the car. The motor started immediately. He levered the selector into low and floored the accelerator. The four-barrel carburetor moaned and the rear tires laid a long pair of loud black marks through a sliding U-turn out of the service station and onto the pavement west. The fan belt didn't squeak.

The kid stood in the acrid blue smoke under the moths and the lights, thirty dollars and a can of brake fluid in his hand, and grinned appreciatively until the Ford's ruby tail lights disappeared over a light rise in the night desert, about two miles away. Then he swung his fist and turned all the way around, making a fast car noise with his voice.

On the telephone, Emmy Cohen had told Windrow some very disturbing, though not unexpected news. To wit: she had discovered the terms of O'Ryan's will.

· Leaving monies to his various foundations and charitable enterprises, with generous sums remaindered to Hardpan and Sal, everything else went to Jodie.

Windrow didn't know what to make of it. He'd thought there'd been a pattern in the slaughter; thought that there might even be reason to believe that someone had killed old man O'Ryan—although it could never be proven: Woodruff might almost wear the shirt of guilt, with a little tailoring, if he lived long enough to try it on.

Again and again his mind swerved from what most of it wanted to think. Again and again, that part of it that had brought him to his senses, sitting on the staircase of his office building, returned him to the one fact he'd withheld from Bdeniowitz, the fact he hadn't allowed himself to admit to anyone.

After he'd stumbled over the body of Concepción Alvarez, turned on the light, examined her, searched his office and called the police, he'd gone for a drink. The ice had been in the freezer, in the top of the old refrigerator. As it had done several times in the past week, his eye drifted up to linger over the guitar case Jodie had left behind when Sal had come to get her.

This time, going for the ice had been no different. His mind was on the body on the floor behind him when, replacing the tray in the freezer, his eyes checked the top of the refrigerator. It had taken a second, maybe two, for the vacancy to register.

The instrument was gone.

Now, blazing into the tunnel in the desert night burrowed by his headlights, he felt again that tingling in his sternum that had spread to his churning stomach, causing him to harden his jaw as he stood in front of the refrigerator, the light from the icebox on his face, a corpse on the floor behind him, the sensation presaging an inevitable and terrible conclusion.

Staring into the highway illuminated by his high beams he missed the turnoff to Reward. He slammed on his brakes and, in the hundred yards it took him to stop, almost missed McKittrick. The five or six buildings McKittrick contained were completely dark, lit only by the wild swing of his headlights as he turned around and swung onto the dirt road that went toward Reward.

Gas flares threw lurid, erratic shadows into the sky above the hills around him. Clusters of lights and jets of steam appeared here and there in the desert, far off the road. A walking beam pump, nodding in and out of its inexorable chore to pull the oil to the surface, appeared in his lights and disappeared as he passed. He passed several others, traveling perhaps three or four miles until he came to a crossroad. He turned right, driving slowly. The road was rough; the tail of the Ford dragged after each bump. Five miles further a jeep track angled off the road to the left, skewed between him and a fenced-in pump, came back to the road again and then veered sharply to the left and disappeared into the night.

Windrow stopped the Ford and killed its lights, ignoring a pair of unblinking yellow eyes that watched him from beneath an atroplex.

Slowly, his own eyes got used to the darkness, and he found he could make out a vast arrangement of stars overhead, stretching from horizon to horizon in the north and south. Toward the west, the Temblor Range pitched a silhouette of darkness against a few degrees of sky and to the east the several oil fields diffused enough light into the dust above them to effectively obscure the starlight beyond.

When his eyes were completely adjusted, Windrow backed the Ford without lights down the jeep track and parked it on the side of the fenced pump opposite the road.

Sitting on the edge of the opened trunk, he put on an old pair of waffle-soled walking shoes, dark denim pants, a couple of heavy cotton shirts, and a canvas hunting vest.

He emptied his pockets into the trunk of the Ford, keeping only the car key, which he put into the watch pocket of the denim pants. A pocket knife, a flashlight and his .38, went into pockets, in the vest, and he closed the trunk lid.

Then he waited for a while.

The air was very cool and very clear. Watching the desert oil complexes around him, he would sometimes see fire leap out of a vertical flare pipe, like dragon breath, as it suddenly received more fuel; a couple of seconds later he would hear it. Behind him, the electric motor running the walking beam whirred quietly.

He walked around the fence until he came to a sign that hung off its gate. The moon was only a week or so past full, and it provided plenty of light for him to read

O'RYAN PETROLEUM
JODIE 9
KEEP OUT

He came back to the side of the fence against which the Ford was parked and scanned the desert to the northwest, the direction in which the jeep track disappeared, until he saw what he was looking for. The rise of the Temblors beyond made the world dark over there, but the waning moon was straight up, and Windrow could make out the silhouette of a shack against the hills.

He'd wanted to avoid using the thin jeep road, but a few minutes of walking beside it convinced him otherwise. The desert floor was continually cut by narrow gullies and washes, gravel deposits, and holes of every size and description. He knew it was too late in the year for most rattlesnakes to be awake, but a twisted knee or ankle at this stage of the game would be decidedly inconvenient. He decided to risk the jeep road and returned to it.

The shack seemed to be a few miles distant, and the jeep road didn't go straight to it, but rather meandered from well to well in that general direction. An hour later he'd passed three more wells, Jodies 7, 5, and 4, and was squatting on his heels watching a jet, flying high and fast, north to south, when he saw lights swerve across the desert floor.

A car, driving recklessly, was making its way down the first dirt track off the Reward road. As it approached the pump behind which the Ford was hidden, Windrow thought the car was travelling so fast that it couldn't make the turn, if it was going where he was going.

But it did. The headlights swung an arc far to the left, then too far to the right, left again, then straight, bounding up and down. The driver was definitely driving too fast for the jeep track, constantly in a controlled slide.

Though still at least a couple of miles away, Windrow slunk to a gully about fifty yards off the road and lay down in it. The short trip off the road had covered his boots and socks with foxtails. So he idly picked them out of his clothing, one by one, as he lay watching and listening.

Soon he heard the slough of tires in sand, the chassis of

the car banging into its body, its rear bumper and differential bouncing off the center of the road. The bucking vehicle and its wild lights passed Windrow's hiding place spewing sand, and wound further into the desert. It was the Chevy wagon. The same vehicle in which he had seen the woman wearing the eighth-note haircomb. He cautiously raised his head and followed its progress. Soon he could no longer hear it, only see its lights, and a while later the lights of the car swung to illuminate a fence with a beam lifting above it, a car beside the fence, the side of the building next to that, before they extinguished. A pall of dust raised by the car diffused moonlight for more than a mile back along the road from the house toward Windrow.

That would be O'Ryan's desert home, and Windrow would want to be talking to the driver of the Chevy.

He made his way back to the road, then jogged fifty paces and walked fifty paces until, fifteen minutes later, he was within a hundred yards of the house. There he squatted behind a tall creosote bush until the pounding in his head and chest had subsided, watching the shack. The wagon sat in front of it, empty. He saw no one.

Crouching from bush to bush, .38 in hand, he made his way to the side of the pump fence. Here he paused again. Through the links in the fence, when the beam raised, he could see a chink of light between the sash of a window and whatever had been used to cover the rest of the glass. He moved to the front corner of the fence and looked at the windows of the house facing the porch. These too, had been masked from within, and only some small bits of light escaped through holes or cracks.

Between the house and the pump stood a venerable Cadillac. All its tires were flat. Windrow made his way to the side of the car away from the house.

In the porch yard, the Chevy Wagonaire waited. Both front doors stood open, and its cooling motor snapped and creaked.

Silently, Windrow made his way to the quarter panel on this car, getting a look at its license plate on his way by. California, GUSH.

Windrow hesitated. Two open doors on the car indicated that there could be at least two people inside the house. Of course, the driver might have been by himself, and merely unloaded something from the right side.

He thought he should wait to see what developed, as he worked his crouch around the outside of the car, around the front end, to the edge of the porch. Yes, that probably was what he should do. Better judgment would indicate that the operative should just wait and see what happened. He took a step onto the porch. He could take one or two people as they came out the door, if he were in the right position, somewhere on the other side of the Chevrolet, for instance. Or he could wait around the side of the building.

He was three steps onto the porch and just two steps from turning the door knob with his free hand when the door opened wide.

Windrow was flooded in light. He squinted and lunged low into the man who had opened the door. The man had been backing out of the house, and he screamed. Windrow grabbed his left arm and twisted it high up between the man's shoulder-blades and yanked him backwards, through the door onto the porch. As he did this he yelled Freeze! Into the man's ear, as loudly as he could, ran his gun arm between the man's right arm and body, and jammed the muzzle of his pistol hard into the hollow between the man's jaw hinge and his neck. All of this caused the man to involuntarily pull the door, which opened inward, toward him, as Windrow pulled him back. Windrow hadn't wanted that. Using his leverage on the man's twisted arm, Windrow pushed him forward, so that the man's face smashed against the closing door and pushed it open again, the door swung wide to the left, banged against the wall upon which it was hinged.

They stood there, in the doorway. By now Windrow knew that the man shaking in his arms was Woodruff, but he had a little more trouble with the other person in the room. He could tell it was a woman, because her clothes were in shreds, and the straight–backed chair she was tied into was facing him, and the only light in the room was a lamp on a table in the corner in front of her, but it seemed like a long time before he realized that, properly rearranged, the swollen and suppurating features on her motionless face would spell Jodie Ryan.

He put all his strength into kicking Manny Woodruff toward a stuffed easy chair, and all his artifice into twisting the arm as he released it, so that it dislocated the shoulder. But it was the shotgun blast from the front door, beside Windrow's ear, the gun behind him, that carried Woodruff over the chair and crashing into the bookcases beyond. Two stout arms expertly landed the barrels of the shotgun on the point of Windrow's right shoulder, numbing his entire right arm. The blow sent his .38 twirling after Woodruff in the yellow lamplight, and the boot planted in Windrow's back sprawled him against the same chair over which poor Woodruff had died in midair.

Silence.

"Sit down," somebody said. Windrow hadn't fallen over the chair, but used his good arm to stop himself. He caught a glimpse of Woodruff, splayed and dead in the shadows under a heap of paperback books, cinder blocks, and board shelving, and a violent odor assailed his nostrils. The arms and legs jutted from the corpse at angles never seen on a live human, there was blood and exposed meat. Windrow, the small hairs on the back of his neck uncurling, righted the chair. Then he slowly turned around.

It might have been a man, who faced him. It dressed like one. Western leisure suit, light green with bright magenta piping that made double vees over the shoulders and breast pockets, nacre buttons on the jacket and shirt, matching green bootcut pants over the expensive, polished but scuffed boots, an olive short-brim Stetson and a very white silk kerchief around the neck, knotted at the throat, it all gave the general appearance of a particular style of manhood, though the brows and lashes of the grey eyes evidenced extraordinary care; but the silver hair, the subtlest hint of bluish tinge and further extraordinary attention showing as it cascaded from the hatsize to the shoulders, where it curled inward toward the neck and upward again before it stopped, trimmed and coiffed just so, indicated a meticulous femininity to Windrow, in spite of the shotgun.

The subject of Windrow's puzzlement now paused to reload this formidable weapon, expertly breaking the breach so that the two spent shells, twelve gauge, dropped smoking out of their chambers to the floor, and inserting two fresh loads, as casually as if their predecessors had just dropped a quail, rather than a man. Windrow measured the distance between himself and the killer, and kept still.

His right ear rang loudly from the shotgun blast, but it was the virulent odor from the fabric of the chair that gradually replaced the pungence of burned powder. A powerful and moving odor, it reminded him of dysentery, live garbage, and dead animals. It was the unmistakable stench of decomposition.

He realized that Sweet Jesus O' Ryan must have died in this chair.

The sounds of breathing that came from the nearly inert form of Jodie Ryan to his right were of air moving erractically through broken and caved-in passages, as of the congested pulmonation of a sleeping, sick child. Her head lay on one shoulder, she was unconscious, retained upright by brown leather straps that held her in her chair. The straps looked to be parts of harness or bridle.

Against the wall beyond her was a pile of additional leather goods, including a riding quirt.

Next to these Windrow spotted a truly curious item. It was an empty wire cage draped in leather straps. There seemed to be other cages behind it.

Windrow returned his gaze to the person with the shotgun, and found that he had been quietly watched by the grey eyes as his own eyes had scanned the contents of the room. The two hands still held the shotgun, and its breach had not been closed.

Windrow smiled and moved the ball of his right foot, so that the boot made a little noise against the floor.

The breach snapped to. The eyes hardened. A smile flitted across the face.

"You'll be Jody Dweem," Windrow said.

Chapter Eighteen

A PLUCKED BROW ARCHED AND FELL.

"How come I'm not dead?" Windrow asked, not without interest.

The two barrels had been aimed at the floor until he'd moved his foot, but they were up now; to Windrow they looked like a pair of water mains being raised by a crane.

The eyes smiled. "Out of bullets, there, for a minute." The voice was a nasty, cultivated drawl.

Windrow moved his head slightly to indicate the body on the floor behind his chair. "Woodruff lose his nerve? Or did he just find out who was doing what to whom?"

The impulse to pull the trigger flirted in the grey eyes, he could see it.

"Or did he finally realize how crazy his partner really is, and what was happening to everybody else was going to happen to him, too -- probably sooner than later?"

Windrow would have liked to let his mind race through the logic of the insanity, over the pieces, past the bodies, beyond the facts, and out the window, preferably with Jodie Ryan, magically. The fantasy had its appeal. The gun level with his face now, straight out from its master's hip, and the smell of corruption coming from the fabric of the chair brought all the fluids to the surface of the walls of Windrow's stomach. He knew if he stared hard enough he would begin to think he could see the noses of the two shells waiting at the other ends of their two gaping conduits. That the muzzle of the gun floated steadily less than ten feet from his face meant that accuracy was a foregone conclusion. Still, there was a slight edge in his favor; in the choice of a long-barreled gun at this range, even if it was sawed off, all he would have to do was move faster than, say, light.

Then again, maybe Dweem would have an epileptic fit and drop the gun.

He concentrated on the eyes.

"Where's Sal?"

The eyes narrowed.

"Out back? In the Bay? In somebody's gas tank?"

The forefinger tightened on the front trigger, the middle finger tightened on the rear trigger.

It's to be both barrels, right in the face. A little voice announced it in Windrow's head. His system flipped to protest the observation, but his mind overrode that decision. He forced the tension to flow out of himself, as if it were a charge draining from his skeleton. The knotted muscles at his clavicle distended, his shoulders lowered immeasurably, his lower jaw moved back into place—even the tiniest hint of a complex smile took command of his lips, and he said, "You never got over O'Ryan going straight and getting rich while he was at it, did you Dweem."

He phrased the remark as a question, but inflected it as a declaration, not as a supposition, but a conclusion, as a matter of scientific fact, as if he were displaying a length of psycho-sociological thread whose characteristics were plain enough for anyone to see.

The eyebrows arched, the eyes narrowed, then flared, and the mouth opened. "Hah!" exploded between the bared teeth. "I didn't think you had it in you." Dweem laughed a short elliptical laugh. The fingers relaxed against the blades of the triggers. "Oh my," he said, chuckling. "Oh my goodness." The gun lowered just a little. "What a tough guy. Mm!" He shook his head. "I'm on the wrong track, here. This isn't going to hurt at all, the way I'm going about it. And after all the trouble you've been to me. Tsk." He clucked his tongue.

Windrow, tense in the apparent reprieve, found himself somewhat gouged by this last remark. "Trouble?" he expostulated, incredulous. "*I* caused *you* a lot of trouble? Where the hell do you get that? If you'd left off killing people this week, I'd still be nursing a sore face through a swimming pool investigation—."

"Sure, sure, honey," Dweem said distractedly, "Is that what you were doing at Pammy-baby's: *cleaning her pool?*"

Windrow's mind began to sound like the room where they keep the relays at the telephone company, clicking all the time.

"You made the phone call."

"*Very* astute."

"Was it to tell Woodruff that Jodie—" Dweem gave Windrow a sharp look at the mention of the name, "that Jodie had gotten away from you long enough to call me?"

Dweem said nothing, but moved toward his left, keeping the gun pointed at Windrow's face. But Windrow had it now, he could feel the story assuming its shape as he told it, his narrative was like blowing air into a nozzle at one end of an inflatable hotel room, and watching all the furniture slowly rise up and assume its shape. Pictures on the wall, the flickering TV, an ashtray with burning cigarette, the bed, the Bible, a lamp. He kept talking.

"That telephone call wasn't planned. Woodruff was in a lather about my arrival until you called. When he told you I was there, talking about a second will nobody knew existed, the two of you cooked up a story to side track me until you could find out what was going on. You knew Jodie had phoned me that morning, and have planned to eliminate me since. But then you jumped the gun. Well, the laugh's on you Dweem. I didn't know boo about a second will. That was just a line to get the Woodruffs to talk to me."

Dweem took another step to his left.

Windrow wiggled the tingling fingers of his right hand. "Lessee, lessee, how'd it go. You found out the terms of the first will after everybody left the cremation in Las Vegas, after Woodruff had gotten Pamela to marry him. It left the works to Jodie, and all bets were off: Pamela was useless, Jodie was hot." He paused, then added carefully. "But you didn't kill Pamela out of frustration. You killed her out of jealousy."

Dweem still facing Windrow, had his back to the three cages. Cocking his right leg behind him, he used the toe of his boot to slide one cage away from the wall. Windrow watched this maneuver, registering the distance between himself and Dweem. Jodie Ryan slumped between them, slightly to Windrow's right, breathing raggedly.

Dweem paused. "Do go on, Mr. Windrow," he said, grimacing pleasantly. "This is a most interesting exegesis—although, I think, you personally will find its confirmation rather... creepy."

Windrow hesitated. The cage Dweem had advanced contained a large grey tarantula. The spider remained motionless on the bottom of the cage, despite its being moved. Windrow thought, rather hopefully, that it may have just arrived from the taxidermist.

As if perceiving this thought, Dweem sat on his heels behind the cage and tickled the spider's behind with one of his fingers. Immediately, the tarantula lowered its head, raise its rear end, and scrubbed itself vigorously with its two back legs. Windrow stared at the spider for a moment, then looked at Dweem, who was watching him.

"Please continue, Mr. Windrow, with your version of the events leading up to this tableau." He chuckled and stood up, adding, "I think that's quite clever, calling this a tableau, don't you? All the players are quite motionless, quite frozen in their respective poses, even down to our friend here, Boris, the hairy mygalomorph, himself." Not taking his eyes from Windrow, Dweem lowered his long eyelashes at the tarantula, which, as he spoke, had ceased to move. "Perhaps the humblest of our ensemble—if not least among us." He sighed. "Poor Woody," he said. "Only I, the director," he drew out the pronunciation of this last word, articulating each syllable, "freely move about the set. All the other players are quite— shall we say—inert?" Dweem stood and crooked one arm under the shotgun.

Windrow drew a breath and continued. "But first, to protect yourself, you tried to kill me. You knew you had a fair chance of getting away with it. No one but Woodruff knew who you were; Sal had already taken a poke at me..." Windrow paused, then said, "That was stupid, Dweem. Just plain stupid. I don't think your decisions are always... rational."

Dweem glowered at him. His eyebrows jerked about like pennants in stormy weather.

"Then, thinking I was dead, you killed the poor Neil woman... Stupid. Have you ever considered your thought process as being irrational? No? How about... deranged?"

Dweem tightened his jaw, but said nothing. With the toe of his boot, he slid a second cage away from the wall, until it was beside the first.

"Lobe was harder. Why? What was it? Did you try to

con him into selling Jodie Ryan's contract to Woodruff? Or directly to you? Probably to yourself, right? And he wouldn't go for it?"

Dweem was silent. He gently tapped the second cage with the toe of his boot: once, twice. The second time, the tarantula in this cage threw itself at the boot toe with such startling alacrity that Windrow involuntarily twitched. He thought that the spider must have sprung six inches straight up from a dead standstill. Again it threw itself at the teasing boot toe, and Windrow noticed that this tarantula was different from the other one. It was entirely covered in coarse hairs like the first, but this spiders' hair was black except for a bright band of halloween orange around the middle of each leg.

Dweem glanced as if modestly through his lashes at Windrow. "Orange-kneed model," he said quietly, "from Mexico. A female. Particularly vicious. I call her Chi-Chi."

Windrow ignored this and took up the thread of his story. "The plan at its simplest stage was to get Jodie's contract from Lobe cheap, then sell it to the highest bidder. Jodie Ryan herself, with her sudden wealth, would be chief among these bidders, of course."

"Of course." muttered Dweem, disappointed in the effect the spider was having on Windrow.

"You might even have offered it to her exclusively."

"Might."

"But that deal was coming unraveled before you even got started, because you needed Pamela Neil's cut of O'Ryan Petroleum to back the purchase. You tried to bluff Lobe anyway, but he probably had similar plans of his own. Then you threatened him. Effectively, too. I saw him. He knew how crazy you are. He was right. You killed him." Windrow shook his head. "Dumb, dumb, Dweem. Dumb."

Dweem looked menacingly at Windrow. Windrow returned the gaze.

"That's what happened, right? When you and Manny went to see Lobe, he wouldn't even give you the time of day. You walked into his office ready to talk deal. You ran some number; you're big time east coast TV connection talking syndication, staff of tunesmiths, satellite uplinks, simulcast holograms on Mars, etcetera. Woodruff is the connection who knows the talent, Jodie Ryan. And the agent, Mr. Lobe, is the key to her future. Everybody's in for a cut, even Jodie. Hah." Windrow waved his hand, his right one. It seemed to help the circulation. Dweem steadied the shotgun. "He laughed you out of the office: Why?"

Dweem scowled. The musculature beneath his skin worked peculiar lines in his features, and Windrow could suddenly see clearly where the plastic surgeon had begun and left off work on Jody Dweem's face.

"Why?" Dweem repeated icily, through clenched teeth.

Windrow almost interrupted the question with the answer. "Because Lobe knew the whole story, top to bottom, before you two turkeys had the car turned around in the street to drive over there. Am I right?"

Dweem abruptly squatted under the leveled shotgun and placed a third cage, the one with the straps, next to the cage containing the orange-kneed tarantula. One end of the cage was hinged. He opened it.

"How did he happen to be in possession of such a hotline? Easy. Pamela Neil bought her cocaine from her maid, Concepción Alvarez, who bought it from Harry Lobe. Everybody knows everybody. It's so simple it makes me feel stupid to think about it."

"Hmph."

"But not for the reasons *you* think it's stupid, you nelley jerk-off," Windrow continued angrily. "Lobe didn't want to play ball, so you used the bomb you brought along to scare him with. You were thinking if he didn't want to sell out cheap enough or not at all, you'd have this goddamn time bomb go off in his wastebasket at three a.m., when nobody was around. He'd get scared enough to sell out. But he was completely hip to your plans because Concepción Alvarez called him up and told him about it. More to the point, he wasn't going to get pushed around by a nelly cowgirl and a pansy art dealer, no matter *what* the deal was. Am I right?"

Dweem curled his lip but said nothing.

"But you still needed his signature. So the bomb must have gone off too early. A mistake. Or was it? Was that when Woodruff noticed how crazy you are? A deal's a deal, right? A little intimidation, a little extortion—that's business. Business is money. But blowing people up because they won't make a deal? That's not business, that's murder, that's insane.

"So you killed Lobe. Then you killed the Alvarez girl. And you killed Pamela Neil, way back into last week. You tried to kill me. You just killed Thurman Manny goddamn Woodruff. You've probably killed Sal. And why? *Why?* For revenge? You killed five goddamn people because they got in the way of your imagination, and in my case, because you only *thought* I was in the way of the way you *thought* things were. You killed five people going on six because they beat you at your own goddamn game, and half of them didn't even know there was a game going on. You're sick, Dweem, STUPID AND SICK—!"

Windrow was ready, but Dweem didn't go for it. He had the shotgun leveled at Windrow, and he was breathing heavily, but he didn't just throw the gun down and try to kill the big-mouth detective with his bare hands, as Windrow hoped he would.

Oh well.

Windrow was shaking. He tried to calm down, and he was thinking clearly enough to notice the numbness in his right arm had gone away. But then he began to talk again. He couldn't help himself. He was quivering with rage. But what difference did it make? The spiders... He knew Dweem had something nasty in mind with them, something extenuated and nightmarish. So the idea was to set Dweem off. Maybe he would make a mistake, a false move, maybe he wouldn't. But, in any case, why not get it over with? Flesh out the sordid little tale in the isolated shack in the vast, unheeding desert until the maniac got infuriated to the point of blasting him into oblivion, to hell with neatness, and to hell with the spiders, too. So Windrow pushed.

"What about old man O'Ryan, Dweem? What was it like, being a gay couple in Texas in 1925? Not all that bad on the ranch, I'll bet. Maybe only a few of the hands knew, eh? On the other hand, maybe the whole crew was gay—yeah, that's it. Talk about a fantasy. Gay caballeros, eh? Lots of fun. You never had to leave the ranch, or when you did it was a big goof fooling the people at the barn dance in total drag. And oh— those slow buggy rides home across the moonlit prairie...

"But then—what happened? O'Ryan go straight? Too tough being queer on the rodeo circuit? Probably not, no. Wait. I got you figured for going soft when the life got too tough. You lost the ranch, the cattle, the boys.... Whose fault was that? Did you blame O'Ryan for the Depression, too? So it got to be a life without money. O'Ryan did alright, riding rodeo. But it was too tough for Dweem, with his soft hands and careful education, his tender feet and tight ass...."

Dweem looked at Windrow with eyes that modulated from pure hatred to sheer malevolence and back again, like a cheap astrological chart. Congruent tones of bluish-grey wafted just beneath the surface of his artificial complexion.

"So you headed for Greenwich Village, or L.A., or Provincetown. Key West? Some place. Anyplace, so long as the life was easier, the scores richer. So long as somebody else was footing the bill. A lot happened to both of you, but one thing for sure: you broke O'Ryan's heart when you left. He couldn't take city life. And you couldn't take work." Windrow sighed a loud fake sigh and turned it into a sneer. "Just two separate... careers, shall we say?

Dweem stared at Windrow a long moment, the shotgun shaking in his hands. Abruptly, he stopped shaking and smiled. Quickly kneeling, keeping the cannon trained on Windrow with the trigger hand, Dweem expertly shuttled the feisty Mexican tarantula out of her cage into the one with the straps and closed the lid. He stood up, holding the cage in one hand and the shotgun in the other, and stepped past Jodie Ryan's rasping body to stand in front of Windrow. He lowered the shotgun until it was aimed at Windrow's crotch.

"This is going to give me a great deal of pleasure, Mr. Windrow," he said. "Even more than when I did it to her." His eyes slid a fraction of a millimeter toward Jodie Ryan and back. He smiled, a thin horizontal smile, a corner of it twitched, and he tilted his head slightly to one side.

"O'Ryan was a silly boy," he said. "He had a knack for winning and losing with equal facility. I wasted my youth on him, let him use me—for what? To live in a plywood trailer behind a pickup truck? He *failed* me. And when he made money again?" He shrugged. "He married a woman." He paused, then screamed. "*A woman!*" Windrow watched him. "I was educated, elegant, beautiful. All I needed was comfort. I couldn't continue without a little, simple comfort. A bath every day, a kitchen... There was no place to *shit* for godsakes...!"

Before Windrow's eyes, the rotted and tortured soul that saturated the fabric of Dweem's body seemed to transude through the sheen of his vanity, leaking out of every pore and imperfectly manicured suture in it, the suppurating osmosis of an unspeakably purulent decay. The strain of the man's corruption suffused and ruined the expensive, painful artifice of the surgeon and the gymnasium, until nothing remained but sodden, nervous machinations, and Dweem's voice trailed to nothing.

Yet, he held the gun.

"I've wandered all over this godforsaken world... When I walked into this room, after fifty years..." His voice cracked, "Edward looked up at me and, he looked up at me and, he, he *croaked. He just died*—right there in that chair! Without a word!"

Dweem's eyes implored Windrow's understanding, but their plea metamorphosed to blame, as if Windrow were somehow responsible for the difficulties behind them; as if, indeed, Windrow himself had perpetrated the horrible trail of death that led to this small building in the desert, and now, somehow, Dweem had become the righteous avenger.

"Like Argos," Dweem muttered, as if to confirm this thought. He skewed his lower jaw, his open mouth formed and deformed odd shapes. "You don't even know what I'm talking about, you ignorant fuck," he hissed. "Odysseus' dog, Argos. When after twenty years Odysseus returned home, the dog took one look, recognized his master, whimpered and died." He gestured with the cage. "*Mr*. Windrow," he sneered, "have you ever read Orwell's *1984, Mr*. Windrow, forget Homer?" He barked a chopped, mirthless laugh, and answered his own question. "No, of course not. You're an ignorant fuck." He reiterated this idea, as if now reinforced in the opinion. "Ignorant fuck." He gestured toward Jodie Ryan, to his left, with the cage, not taking his eyes off Windrow. "*She* had read it," he said. "I watched an entire day of exquisite torture induced upon her by her own imagination after I merely showed her this, and made a slight reference to Orwell." He twisted the cage so that its lid faced Windrow, the hinge on the bottom. A strap dangled off the left edge of the cage, made a loop and came back to the right edge. A second strap came off the top of the cage, just behind the latch, its other end was stitched to the middle of the loop. Each had an adjustable buckle.

"You put it on like a mask, Mr. Windrow, so that the open end of the cage encircles your face."

Windrow looked at the grey eyes in the artificially smoothed face and tilted his head a little, raising an eyebrow.

"Oh yeah?"

Dweem lowered the gun again, until it pointed at Windrow's crotch.

"Or I blow your pelvis through the bottom of that chair, Mr. Windrow, and you bleed to death in about two hours."

Windrow lowered his eyes to the cage.

"Take it."

He hooked his right thumb through the loop and placed the fingertips of his left hand under the sheet-metal bottom. Dweem removed his hands.

Dweem had the butt of the shotgun rested against his right hip, the breach and triggers in his right hand. He held his left hand away from his body, palm down, its arm floating as if for balance, as if he were walking a tightrope. Now, still

in front of Windrow, he backed up a step and tilted the shotgun so that the very end of its pair of short barrels rapped
the bottom of the cage. The tarantula spun to face Dweem.

"Open the lid first, Mr. Windrow. Then put it on
quickly—or you are emasculated."

So silent was the pause that followed this instruction
that Windrow thought he could hear the world turning, and
the rush of its atmosphere in his ears. A drop of perspiration
fell from his armpit onto his upper ribcage, and his stomach
twisted a little tighter against the stench exuded by the chair.
His right ear rang mercilessly.

"You know what that means?"

Dweem jabbed sharply and accurately at Windrow's pelvis with the muzzle of the shotgun. Pain rose into Windrow's
abdomen. "Do it," Dweem hissed.

Windrow slipped the metal clasp and eased the door
open.

The spider turned again.

He had to hold the cage away from his face to allow the
door to drop all the way, until he'd carefully folded it under
the bottom of the cage, where he pinned it with his thumb.

The tarantula, easily as big as one of Windrow's hands,
stood not two inches from the hinge, on the flat piece of
sheet metal that formed the bottom of the cage. Its knees,
Windrow observed, were a very bright orange. They buzzed
with the color. Its mouth and jaws facing Windrow were as
big as his two thumbs would be if held together.

Without warning the spider suddenly crouched its rear
legs.

"You did this to her?" Windrow whispered.

Dweems's voice was tense with excitement. "Only with
the the other spider, the gentler one. It merely... explored
her features... curious, interested in the superficial wounds

I'd earlier inflicted..." He raised the shotgun so that its muzzle was just beyond the back of the cage, pointing through it at Windrow's face. "...She was hysterical, of course...."

Windrow's mouth was dry. Fixing Dweem's eyes with his own, he said, "You'll have to kill her after you kill me, Dweem, now that she's awake."

And for the first time, Dweem took his eyes off Windrow. He turned his head; the grey eyes and the chin under them jerked toward Jodie Ryan, bound to the chair on Dweem's left.

Windrow unwound. As his wrists rotated, his left foot came up and planted its boot against the trigger guard on the shotgun, and he slid his weight under it, toward Dweem, dropping his head beneath the line of fire. His right foot came up too, but caught the shotgun much higher up, toward the end of the length of its short barrels away from the trigger guard. Dweem's eyes came back to see what was happening, his face not far behind, and what they saw was the bottom of the tarantula, as the spider, flipped by the snap of Windrow's wrist out of the mouth of the open cage, landed on Dweem's face. Two of the legs hooked the corner of his opening mouth, and another stabbed into the tear duct of his right eye.

He'd been opening his mouth to scream and his scream was well on its way past the larynx, pushing his tongue before it, out of his throat. But its sound was overwhelmed by the roar of the shotgun. The two barrels discharged their loads straight up, the triggers squeezed by Dweem's convulsing fingers, and the detonations sheared Dweems's expensive face clean out from under the tarantula. The spider dropped, unharmed, to Windrow's knee. It landed lightly, on its feet, like a cat.

Dweem's faceless body floated, the feet rising up until just the toes pointed straight down, its limbs stretched full length, and collapsed backwards to the floor. The shotgun lay clasped in his arms on top of him like a commemorative lily, in much the same position as when it fired.

Something dripped from the cavity in the ceiling.

Windrow considered the mess. He thought it had been the easiest thing he'd done in a long time.

He began to shiver, as if chilled.

Then the tarantula bit him. The effect was of a charged electrode applied to the dimple next to his kneecap. He brushed it to the floor.

Windrow applied a waffled boot to the spider.

That was easy, too.

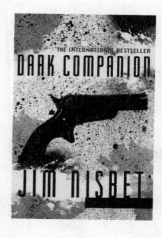

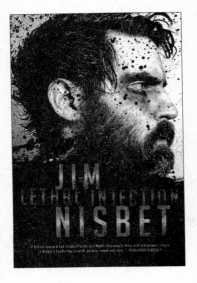